THE LAST FIRST GAME

A COLLEGE ROMANCE

GINA AZZI

A NOTE ABOUT THE LAST FIRST GAME

The Last First Game is a coming-of-age, contemporary sports romance that includes sensitive themes. It is intended for mature audiences.

The Last First Game was formerly published as part of The Senior Semester Series. It has been re-edited and revamped with new content and a fresh look.

THE COLLEGE PACT SERIES

Four best friends.
Four sexy athletes.
Four hot romances.
One college pact!

The Last First Game (Lila's Story)
All the While (Maura's Story)
Me + You (Emma's Story)
Kiss Me Goodnight in Rome (Mia's Story)

AUGUST

PROLOGUE

Lila

The pact is my idea. As soon as it pops into my mind, I recognize its merit. Perched around a café table overlooking Central Park, my three best friends and I munch on chips and salsa and sip Sangria for the last time.

Tomorrow, everything changes.

Clapping my hands together, I secure the attention of my friends. "I have the best idea. Ever."

Emma's face lights up like a Christmas tree, eager for whatever crazy idea I'm going to propose. But the pact is different. It's smart and practical. Exciting yet necessary. It's a way to embrace our senior year of college while reducing the distance between us as we all embark on solo adventures.

"We're waiting." Maura leans back in her chair, plucking at her tank top as the hot August air circles around us.

"This is it, our senior year. After this, we'll be clocking long working hours, trying to climb some proverbial ladder, and spending our weekends doing laundry and meal prep."

"You're depressing as hell sometimes, you know that?" Maura shifts in her seat, elbowing my forearm off the table.

"I'm working up to my pitch."

"Get to the point," she yawns, but curiosity hums in the undercurrent of her tone.

"Senior year is supposed to be fun and wild. Carefree and epic. We're all starting something new, with Mia heading to Rome tomorrow morning."

Maura coughs into her hand but I ignore her. While Mia, Emma, and me are leaving campus this semester, Maura is heading back to McShain University to join her rowing team, same as she's done for the past three years.

Emma, the friend I can count on, nods, her bangs falling into her eyes. "Li is right. We need to turn up this semester."

"Exactly. So, I'm proposing a pact." I pause to swallow a large gulp of sangria.

"A pact?" Mia quirks an eyebrow. "Like what?"

"We need to date hotties, the sexy kind who stop existing once we graduate. You know how it goes, guys start working, stop working out, and let their shit go."

Emma snorts. "And have wild nights out, getting stupidly drunk with strangers. Those are always the best stories."

"Make new friends?" Mia glances at the rest of us. Always the prima ballerina, I question if she's ever dipped one toe out of her comfort zone.

"Fine," Maura grumbles, "but since you're all leaving me, I want weekly updates and photos."

Mia grins, her chocolate brown eyes shimmering as dusk falls. "So, we'll keep in touch."

"All the time," I swat a gnat away from the two pizzas our server deposited in the center of our table. "We update each other on everything going on and we swear that for this semester, we go all out: break the barriers, bend the rules, and live the hell out of our college experience. No stressing about grades and exams. No falling in love and dealing with serious relationship drama. Just wild, fun, good times. Mia, you're going to Rome tomorrow. Travel, eat everything, make out with all the tall, dark, and handsomes. Emma, I expect nothing less than gossip and scandal and midnight liaisons in the Capitol building."

"Done." Emma wiggles her eyebrows, breaking off a piece of pizza crust and popping it into her mouth.

"Maura, damn girl, the past few months have sucked for you."

A blanket of silence stretches over our table.

"What? I'm not going to sugarcoat it." Reaching out, I wrap my fingers around Maura's wrist and squeeze. "This semester is a fresh start. Don't waste it. Just do you and focus on yourself, your healing. Maybe rowing will help."

Maura's eyes narrow, two black orbs of anger.

"Maybe it won't." I gentle my tone. "It's okay if you're done with rowing. But you need to figure that out for yourself. Do you."

"What about you, Li?" Mia asks, releasing Maura from the hot seat.

"I'm about to go to Cali." I flutter my eyelashes. "Screw this stupid internship program. This semester, I'm all about a hot surfer with blond hair and blue eyes. While you bitches are busting your asses, I'm going to lie on a beach all day, soak in some rays, and drink colorful beverages with tiny umbrellas." Standing, I twirl at the edge of our table, my skirt billowing out around the tops of my thighs.

Emma smacks my ass. "Stop with the stereotypes or you won't make any new friends. Your program isn't even near the beach."

"I'm dreaming, babe. And that's my point, that's what this semester should be about."

"Making our dreams come true?" Maura snorts, cynicism lacing her tone.

Glancing around the table, a pause hovers between us until we all erupt in laughter, like a water balloon bursting. "Okay, fine, that part was cheesy," I admit.

Grinning at my friends, I drink in their idiosyncrasies one last time. Over the past three years of living together, they're closer to me than sisters. A pang of longing hits me square in the chest; how am I going to survive this semester without them?

"Okay." Emma raises her sangria. "To adventure, hot boys, and an epic senior year."

"To our college pact," I add.

We raise our glasses, look each other directly in the eye as we clink our sangrias together. "Cheers!"

SEPTEMBER

1

CADE

"Hey." Answering my cell, I lean back in my seat near gate A24.

"Yo, dude. What time do you land?" my best friend, Miers, asks.

"Around 3PM." I toss my wallet and boarding pass into my carry on. Stretching my legs out, a soreness throbs in my right knee and I shift forward to massage the tender joint. "What're you up to?"

"Kicking it now but we're doing wings for dinner tonight."

"Sweet, I'll be there. How was practice today?"

Miers sighs and I clutch my phone tighter to my ear.

"It was okay but not great. We play Arizona U in eight days and honestly, Cade, I'm not sure if we're ready for them. If we don't start our season with the right momentum and morale, it's going to suck. Mullins filled in for you today, but Coach is eager to have you back."

"Yeah." I clear my throat. "It was cool of Coach to let me fly home this weekend."

Silence hangs on the line between us and I pluck at the

skin next to my right eye. "I'm fine, man," I answer Miers's unasked question.

He clears his throat and I imagine him removing his baseball hat and placing it back on his head the way he does when he's uncertain. "You sure?"

"Yep."

"How was the memorial service?"

"Nice."

"And being home?"

"Shitty," I admit. "He's everywhere. Hell, my mama hasn't even touched his room. It's exactly as he left it the morning he shipped out for boot camp." This weekend, I dreaded the suffocating walls of my childhood home in New Jersey, struggling to breathe against the influx of memories that center on my brother: tossing the pigskin in the backyard, washing Dad's car in the driveway during summer. Jared's death in Iraq last year—IED roadside explosion—was the worst day of my life.

His one-year memorial service was second.

"Sorry, dude. That shit is heavy. You know if you need anything…" Miers trails off.

"I'm good."

"Alright, well, hit me up when you land. I'll make sure we order extra garlic wings."

Recognizing Miers's offer as sympathetic, I hang my head. Dude's not big on words but he's old school and his actions always speak louder. "Thanks."

"Safe travels, thirty-three." He references my jersey number before hanging up.

Slipping my phone back into the pocket of my jeans, I scan the airport. As usual, it's bustling with business people rocking crisp suits and rolling compact luggage, the gait of college kids slumped under backpacks, and the tear-stained faces of toddlers who skipped their naps.

But damn. Hold up.

The entire airport disappears as I zero in on *her*.

She's straight-up fierce, commanding the space around her, and coloring the air with her energy. Tall and blonde, with a sexy sashay to her hips, she's oblivious to the looks every person, male and female, toss in her direction.

Waltzing past me, she blows her hair out of her eyes, and slides her shoulder bag onto a chair a few seats away from mine. Pulling her oversized cardigan around her slim frame, she perches on the edge of her seat, her foot tapping against the ground. Cardigan girl sips her coffee, glancing around the airport until her gaze slams into mine.

Holy shit.

Her eyes are the most unique shade of cornflower blue, like cloudless summer skies somewhere in the Midwest. Not that I've ever been to the Midwest to know firsthand, but this girl rocks that wholesome, innocent look, like she's traveling from some podunk *Little House on the Prairie* village. But that's where the resemblance ends. She may look sweet and wholesome, but her personality screams fearless. She oozes confidence, as evidenced by her glare before she looks past me, breaking our connection.

Chuckling, I check her out. Hard. Mainly because she's not the type of woman any red-blooded male looks away from. But also because in my last three years of playing Division I football, I don't think a woman has ever brushed me off so casually, like flicking at a gnat buzzing around her head.

"Excuse me?" An airline representative approaches her.

She glances up, crosses one knee over the other, and smiles. "Yes?"

And Jesus, it's a transformative experience. My brain

short-circuits as I drink in her smile, my eyes tracing the curve of her full bottom lip. Her voice has a raspy pull to it, one that draws me closer in hopes of hearing it again.

"I'm sorry to interrupt you. It seems this flight is overbooked. For customers willing to wait until the next flight to Los Angeles, which departs in three hours, we are offering a free round-trip ticket to be used within one year of today's date. Would you be willing to give up your seat on this flight and take the next flight?"

Cardigan Girl looks startled, her eyes wide. Like a creeper, I can't tear my eyes away. She's too damn enticing, and I hang on to the words falling from her mouth. "Sure. Is the flight anywhere in the network or only JFK-LAX?"

Beautiful, badass, and intelligent. Cardigan Girl is the damn trifecta.

"JFK-LAX."

"Okay. That's fine."

The airline representative points to the desk near the gate. "My colleague will assist you at the desk. Thank you for your understanding and cooperation. And thank you for flying with us today."

Cardigan Girl stands and stretches her arms overhead. Her cardigan is oversized, hanging to her knees, but the T-shirt underneath clings to her like a second skin, showing off her wicked curves. Shouldering her bag, she turns toward the desk.

The guy sitting next to me clears his throat and gives me a pointed look. Grinning back, I shake my head. I should feel embarrassed for checking CG out so hard. I should feel stupid for being called on it by the sixty-year-old dude next to me. But all I feel is grateful that I'm going to kick it with this girl for the next three hours.

The eagerness I felt about getting back to LA disappears.

Now, catching the next flight to LA seems less like capital punishment and more like an opportunity. Possibility crackles in the air around me, spurring me into action.

Pulling out my phone, I text Miers.

Me: Flight delayed. Be back late.

"Excuse me. Miss?" I call out to the representative.

She turns and I grin, sauntering to my feet. "I couldn't help but overhear you," I begin, flexing my bicep for extra incentive.

The man next to me groans.

Ignoring him, I focus on charming the airline representative the same way I talk my way out of mandatory study halls, "but if you need additional customers to give up their seats, I have no problem taking the next flight."

2

LILA

"A Heineken, please." Climbing onto a bar stool, I drop my oversized bag to the floor. Obviously, I over-packed, but that was a given.

"Here you go." The bartender places a pint of Heineken on a coaster next to my hand.

"Thanks." I push a twenty-dollar bill across the bar and take a large gulp of my beer, the lager cool and refreshing.

Glancing at my phone, a Snapchat from Mia pops up. Clicking on her handle, MammaMiaP, her face appears with a giant cone of gelato, bits of cream evident on her face. "Nice." Muttering to myself, I snap a photo of my Heineken, and send it back. *Caption: gearing up for sexy surfers.*

"Mind if I join you?"

Swiveling on the bar stool, I lock eyes with one of the hottest guys I've ever seen. My fingers grip my Heineken. It's the gorgeous guy who checked me out at the gate. Hard. Having his intense eyes scan my face was unnerving; it's like he could see into me, strip away layer by layer, from the moment our eyes met.

And now, here he is.

And wow, he is all the things.

Towering over me, his hard muscles bunch and roll as he shifts his weight. Rich and creamy skin, a shade lighter than cappuccino, dark curls cropped short, nearly to his scalp, and a jawline like a razor's edge, he's got swagger. A confidence that is more than just his looks.

Awareness hums in my veins, warming my blood. Tearing my eyes away from him, flustered by his interest in me, I nod. "Sure. You get bumped as well?"

"Something like that." He lowers himself onto the barstool and a shiver skates up my spine. His eyes are dark gray, heady and expressive, like a thunder cloud in the moments before a rainstorm. Real talk: they're sexy as hell. He's sexy as hell. He must be an athlete. Regular college dudes don't look like this guy. Hell, underwear models don't look like him either.

The space between us charges with an electricity that wasn't there before and I bite the corner of my mouth, hyper aware of every swivel he makes on the barstool. "What're you drinking?" His voice is rough and raspy, and it drags over my skin, like wet sand mixed with gravel.

"A Heineken."

"I'll have the same. Thanks man." He says to the bartender, shifting his weight on the barstool like it's uncomfortable, like it can't support his giant frame. His hands are splayed flat on the bar's surface, the blunt edge of fingertips tapping softly.

Leaning forward, his biceps ripple underneath his dark gray T-shirt and a pair of dog tags swings forward. He looks away as he tucks them back into his shirt, his shoulder blades stiffening.

"Cheers." He holds his pint up to me when his beer arrives.

"Cheers," I echo, clinking my glass against his.

"It's pretty good." He clears his throat, surprise coloring his tone.

"Not normally a Heineken drinker?"

"Nah, more of a Guinness man. But I'm pleasantly surprised."

"It's the smiling E's."

"The what?" He chuckles, tilting his head to gage if I'm playing with him. The corners of his mouth tick up and I grin, way too eager to make this man smirk. Or laugh. Or anything, really.

"The smiling E's." I point to the three e's in Heineken. "See how they're sort of winking at you?"

He studies the lettering, his expression growing thoughtful even though a smirk still hugs his lips. "Yeah, I see it," he admits, a laugh wrapping around his words. "So, what, these smiling E's elevate the beer's taste?"

"Totally." I take another pull from my glass, smacking my lips together. "Their presence makes everything better. Rounds it all out."

Hottie with the body snorts, swiveling on his barstool. Our knees tap once, twice, three times as he twists back and forth and a zing sparks through me, my head buzzing from his proximity. "Are you a beer guru or something?"

"Nah. I don't even really like beer."

"Then why're you drinking it?"

"Because of the e's." I lift my chin at him, widening my eyes like my reasoning should be obvious. "A few years ago, I went to Amsterdam with my brother. We did the Heineken Experience. I loved it so much, I sort of became a brand loyalist."

Angling his body closer to mine, his expression is a

mixture of disbelief and amusement. "Okay. I'm gonna go with it; I feel your logic."

Swiping my tongue across my upper lip to catch the foam, I introduce myself. "I'm Lila."

"Cade. Good to meet you."

"You too. Cade," I add, rolling his name around in my mouth, hoping it's one I repeat in the future.

"You going back to school?" He kicks lightly at my bag on the floor.

"Eh, kind of. I'm doing an internship through Astor for the semester. I really go to college in Philly."

He studies me for a moment, rolling his lips together. "Your version of study abroad?"

"Yes. What about you?"

"I'm a student at Astor. A senior."

"Oh my God, really? Me too. I mean, I'm a senior. I just thought you were older. Maybe in grad school or something."

"Nah. Twenty-two."

"You got me beat then. I'm still twenty-one."

"Old enough to drink. And not just in Amsterdam."

"Thank God for that."

"Kind of tough to miss a semester of your senior year, isn't it?" he asks, raising his beer to his lips.

And wow, to be just one little drop of Heineken in this moment...

"Yeah, I guess so. Although the timing worked out. Two of my best friends left campus for the semester. Mia landed in Rome a few days ago to study abroad and Emma took an internship on Capitol Hill in D.C. Poor Maura, though. She's all by herself on campus, cursing the rest of us."

He glances at me from the corner of his eye, nodding once. "Yeah, that would be tough. Maybe she'll visit you?"

"Or I can visit her. That's why I took the plane ticket. I'm sure I'll want to come back sometime during the semester for a visit."

"Makes sense. So, you're from around here?"

"Sort of. I was born and raised in Massachusetts, but my family moved to New York a few years ago. So, I guess this is home now. What about you?"

"New Jersey. Born and bred."

"A Jersey boy, huh?" I croon the lyrics to "Walk Like A Man" by *The Four Seasons*.

Cade chuckles. "You know, a few years back, everyone had jokes because of *Jersey Shore*. You cracking on me because of *Jersey Boys* is actually a relief."

Grinning, I reach out and squeeze his wrist. Electricity explodes in my fingertips from where my skin grazes his, traveling up my arm and through my body like a live wire. Pulling my hand back, I cover up my reaction with a snicker. "My mom dragged me to see Jersey Boys on Broadway, like, three times," I admit, my mind still caught on how much Cade affects me. How one tiny touch feels so intense, so overwhelming.

"Well, I'm completely tone-deaf so don't get any ideas."

"Noted."

"Do you know anyone in your internship program?"

I sigh, wrapping my fingers around my pint glass so I'm not tempted to touch him again. "Not yet. It's like freshman year all over again. Jitters and orientation and a new roommate."

"Seriously? You're a little badass." He bumps his shoulder against mine and places his beer on the bar, his eyes narrowing in on my lips. "I'll give you my number before we board. I can introduce you to some people on campus. And my house has parties all the time, so you'll have to come by and kick it."

"Your house? I didn't peg you as a frat guy."

Cade tips his head back, his Adam's apple bobbing with laughter. A low, lazy rumble works its way up from his chest as he shakes his head. "Hell no. Nothing against Greek life but it's not my scene. I play football. A bunch of us live together so the house is a guaranteed good time."

Whoa. An Astor football player. Those guys are like campus royalty. Or deities. Take your pick. "Oh, wow, you must be pretty good then."

"Why do you say that?" His eyes glimmer and I can tell he's sucking in a grin, knowing damn straight that Astor only recruits talent. At least, that's what my brother Brandon told me when I accepted the internship.

"Weren't two players from your team drafted at the end of last season? And one of them was only a sophomore."

"Yep. Samson and Hux. So, you're a football fan then?"

"The same way I'm a beer drinker."

He grins, amusement rippling over his face. But curiosity flares in his dark eyes, his elbow glancing off my forearm as he leans closer. "Who's your team?"

"The Patriots."

"What?" he groans. "It's because of Tom Brady, isn't it?"

Breathing in the spice of his cologne, I hold it in my lungs, let it unfurl in my veins and travel through my body like smoke. Cade's presence is heady, and I could easily get drunk off his company, beer or no beer. Shaking my head, I point a finger at him. "That's an unfair assumption."

He holds his hands up in surrender, but I don't buy it for a second. His eyes gleam, brightening a shade to pewter, silver ringing the outer edges of his irises. "Alright, tell me why you chose the Patriots then?"

"I used to watch them with my dad," I admit, the memory slicing at something in my chest. Picking up my glass, I take

a long drink, the tang of beer distracting me from the opera-
tive words in that sentence: *used to*.

Sensing the change in my mood, Cade shifts, his arm
brushing against mine. "I like your answer better than Tom
Brady. Even though I can't fault the guy."

"No one can." I scan his broad chest, noting how his
biceps bulge like two watermelons. "Football suits you a hell
of a lot more than Greek life."

His easy grin is back as he lifts his chin in my direction.
"That's a relief to hear."

I smile.

"So, since we're going to kick it in Cali, we may as well
celebrate the start of senior year together. We've got..." he
pauses, checking his watch "...two more hours to kill."

"Done," I accept, twisting my bar stool even closer to his.
"What are you thinking?"

"Two shots of Patron, please," he calls out to the
bartender.

"Tequila's my favorite."

His eyes flick to mine again, dropping to my lips and
staying there longer than necessary. Heat crawls up my neck
at his intensity and the space between us crackles with
awareness.

"Mine too." His words are soft, fluttering across my skin
on his breath, as if he is sharing something greater than his
preference for mezcal.

The bartender pours two shots and pushes over a salt-
shaker and some limes. Licking my wrist, I shake on some
salt.

"Welcome to Astor, Lila." Cade raises his shot glass.

"Happy senior year, Cade."

We clink our glasses together and lick the salt from our
wrists. Our eyes catch and the heat that flares in his does

things to me, things that normally don't happen. My skin grows hot under his gaze, flushed. My breath sticks in my throat, causing me to cough on my tequila shot.

Reaching out, Cade swipes his thumb over the corner of my mouth, brushing away some salt. Still, I lean into his touch, drawn to him way more than I should be. Way more than this casual exchange calls for.

I focus on the storm brewing in his stare, my lips automatically parting for the lime he holds up to my mouth. Biting into the wedge, the tangy sour taste bursts, and my mind latches onto it, so I can lose myself in this memory again and again.

3

CADE

"Here you go." I pull Lila's suitcase off the baggage carousel and place it in front of her. "Are you sure you can handle all these bags?"

"Oh yeah. This ... pshh." She waves a hand to indicate the assorted pieces of baggage around her feet. "Piece of cake."

"Yeah, okay." Swinging my duffle bag over my shoulder, I stoop and pick up two of her bags, walking toward the exit.

"You're the best." She sing-songs, pulling out a pair of sunglasses and propping them on her nose.

The dry heat hits us immediately, a welcome change from the dense humidity of Jersey.

"Jesus, it's hot."

"Welcome to California. Want to split a cab to campus? That way, you'll end up in the right place and it won't be too expensive." I bite my tongue, my insides sinking. What the hell am I doing? I don't offer to ride share, don't worry if a random girl I just met signs in at the right orientation table.

Waiting for her to respond, I'm half-hoping she says no

just so I can clear her from my head. Her coconut-infused shampoo, the high arch of her cheekbones, hot pink polish on her toenails, all of it is messing with me. She's alluring all right, and I'm the moron falling for her easy smile and casual conversation when I know better.

Keep your guard up. No distractions.

I can already tell that Lila is going to be a giant distraction this semester if I don't screw my head on right. Sure, she's fun and flirty. Fine, she makes my head buzz and my fingers itch to touch her skin. But I'm Cade Wilkins, Astor University running back and a projected NFL draft pick. Women trip over themselves, and each other, clamoring for my attention.

That's why you like this girl. She's not clamoring for jack shit.

"Yeah, that sounds good." She flips her hair over her shoulder and steps in front of me, approaching the taxi stand. I zero in on her ass and groan, noting the seductive sashay of her hips as she walks. I want to reach out and grip the tips of her hair where it brushes against the swell of her ass, dig my fingers into the flare of her hips. In just a handful of hours, I already want Lila underneath me more than I've wanted all of the girls of my first three years of college combined.

And that's a huge problem.

Unaccustomed to the need simmering in my bloodstream, blazing into a full flame when Lila bends down to scratch her ankle, I grasp at my rules. The ones I've stuck to religiously the last two and a half years because football player…and female traps. After a pregnancy scare my freshman year, I axed the notion of serious commitment, preferring to control my dating life and the women I hook up with.

It's too dangerous for an athlete in my position, on the

brink of a professional football career in the NFL, to let every single girl who comes knocking in.

Nope, I practice a casual, no-strings, no commitment, and most importantly, no comments approach to dating. And I already know that Cardigan Girl, *Lila*, is going to challenge the hell out of all of them.

She turns, the sunlight filtering around her, lighting her up like a damn angel. "You coming, Cade?" The undercurrent in her tone pulls at me, spurs me forward, like an invisible thread.

Don't get serious. Don't tangle up. Don't do commitment.
Focus on the game.

It's been my motto since freshman year and I've never been more tempted to push against it. Or ignore it completely.

When Lila's shoulder brushes against my arm as we wait in the taxi line, I crave the electricity that sizzles between us. I'm already intoxicated by her, more interested in her than I am in the dozens of girls who wait for me after a game, who perch on the running boards of my truck, who try to sneak into my house – or bed – any chance they get.

When we're at the front of the line, I spring into action, organizing her luggage and tossing my duffel bag on the middle seat between us, creating a barrier. A physical separation to stop me from reaching out and running my fingers along her wrist or tucking a strand of hair behind her ear.

Slow your roll, thirty-three.

It was one thing to act on my attraction back on the East Coast. There, it was fun and harmless. But I'm back in California now and I can't let myself be swept away by a slamming body and a pair of mesmerizing eyes. Even if they're the most unique shade of blue I've ever seen.

Discussing the beef between two prominent rap artists, the top bars to hit on the Jersey shore, and our favorite plates to order at brunch, the drive to campus passes quickly. Too soon, I'm directing the taxi to her dorm and unloading her bags from the trunk.

"Give me your phone." I beckon with my fingers and she tosses her cell. "I'm adding my number so we can be friends for real." I punch in my number. "Call me if you need anything."

"Thanks for splitting the cab." She reaches into her wallet and begins to remove some bills.

"Get out of here with that."

"No, please." She tries to push a few folded up twenties into my hand.

"Put your money away." I hand her back her phone, my fingers grazing the underside of her wrist. My skin tingles from touching her, pausing over the beat of her pulse. Forcing myself to drop my hand, I clench it into a fist. "Thank you for the educational introduction to Heineken."

Lila laughs, the sound musical and carefree. "You liked that, didn't you?"

"More than I should have. Where are we going?" I gesture toward her bags.

"Oh, it's no worries. I got it from here." Lila picks up one of the shoulder bags and props another on top of her suitcase.

"Let me walk you." I try again, ignoring the grumbling of the taxi driver. *Stop talking. Let her go.*

Unfortunately, Lila hears him and shoots me a worried glance. "I don't want you to lose your ride." She tilts her head, her hair falling forward. "I'll see ya around?"

"Count on it."

"Yo, dude. Why was your flight delayed?" Miers appears in the doorway to my bedroom soon after my arrival home.

"Overbooked. I took the later flight for a free ticket."

"That's all?" he nudges the door open wider with his foot. His six-four frame fills the doorway as he leans against the doorjamb.

"That's all."

"You good?"

"Head's on straight."

"Alright. Well, how're your moms and pops? Did you bring me back anything?"

Digging into my duffle bag, I locate the tin of cookies my mama sent him. Miers is obsessed with mama's cooking, especially her soul food, and she loves having another guy appreciate it. "They're doing alright. Mama sent this for you. Truth, Dad was a bit jealous." I joke, tossing him the tin.

"Nah, your dad adores me. Wishes I was his son." Miers catches the tin and hugs it to his chest like a football, protecting his treats from the guys in the house. It's a necessary precaution because anyone living here would tackle Miers in a heartbeat for some of Mama's chocolate chunk chip cookies.

"Sweet. I'll call her later to thank her." He cracks the lid, his eyes widening at the large cookies resting on a sheet of wax paper. "You feel good for the game?" He removes the lid completely. Taking his first bite of a cookie, he moans and starts dancing in the doorframe.

"Yeah, I think we'll be alright. You know…" I gesture toward the crumbs falling out of his mouth "…it tastes better if you actually chew it. Anyway, sucks about Roberts and Bellans being out for the first game, but I think we can manage without them. At least for now. How's Bellans doing anyway?" I lean back in my desk chair, feigning casual even though I'm concerned for our season opener. We're playing short of the talent we're used to and that's not how I want to start my last season as an Astor athlete.

Miers whistles, shooting more crumbs onto the carpet of my bedroom. "Dude, his shoulder is seriously fucked. I don't know if he's going to come back at all."

"For real?"

"He needs another surgery."

"Damn."

"I know. We can't afford any more injuries. Everyone better stick to conditioning, or we're going to lose before the season starts."

I nod, thinking about Roberts and Bellans. Roberts is one of our best offensive linebackers and Bellans is the second-string QB. Plus, we lost Hux last year when he was drafted.

Miers is still standing in the doorway, chewing. He runs his hand through his shaggy blond hair and eyes me.

"What?"

"Who is she?"

"Who's who?"

"Aw, come on, dude, don't give me that shit. You for sure met someone. Otherwise, you'd be in one hell of a foul mood. You're not moping nearly as much as I anticipated."

"Maybe I'm just dealing."

"Nah. Not your style. You met someone. What's her name? Is she a Jersey girl? Does she rock one of those hair poofs and say things like 'yous'?"

"You really need to never watch *Jersey Shore* again."

"Dude, it's *Jerseylicious*."

"Whatever."

"Don't deflect."

Shaking my head, I ignore my best friend. I just met Lila and if the guys find out I'm crushing on her this hard, the entire house will be busting my balls by practice tomorrow.

My phone chimes with a text and Miers lunges for it, scooping it up from my desk before I can grab it.

"Funny, you don't move that fast in a game."

"Lila, huh?" he tosses me my phone. "I like that name. What's her story?"

"Her story?"

"Yeah. She an East Coast girl? You ever going to see her again?"

I pinch the skin between my eyebrows, struggling to maintain my patience. "I met her at the airport. We both got bumped. Turns out, she's doing a semester here at Astor, some medical internship program."

"Ah, a smarty. Go on."

"She's chill."

"And?"

"And nothing."

"That's it? You're not going to tell me about her ass or that she tried to blow you in the bathroom or…anything?"

Whipping a book at his head, I'm disappointed when he ducks it. "It isn't like that."

Miers whistles low. "Damn, thirty-three. You *like* this chick."

"I barely know her."

"Uh-uh. You like her 'cause you don't want to talk about her."

"That's just being a decent guy."

"Well then I've never witnessed you being decent before now." His shit-eating grin disappears as his eyebrows dip. "Wait, man. Don't go getting all invested in some girl at the start of the season. It's our senior year. You gotta stay focused on the game, on the NFL. You have…

rules." He jabs a finger in my direction as if to punctuate his point.

I flip him the middle finger, kicking my feet up on my desk and stacking one foot on top of the other. A twinge of pain radiates around my kneecap but I ignore it, not wanting to give Miers any more fuel to call me out. "Relax, Miers. She's just a girl I met at the airport. I don't even know her last name."

"That's not saying much."

"She's a cool girl. That's it. How was wing night?"

Miers watches me for another beat before shrugging. "Same as always. James is still on that vegetarian kick so he passed, Hendrix insisted he makes a better buffalo sauce than Anchor's, and Moody's girl ate all the fries while pretending to be on a diet."

"So I didn't miss anything?"

"Not a thing. Come down once you unpack." Miers taps his fist against the doorjamb as he leaves my room. "Mine!" I hear him yell out from the staircase. No doubt, the cookies will be finished before practice tomorrow.

Standing, I kick my bedroom door shut and collapse on my bed, propping my knee up on a pillow. It's swollen, soreness traveling up into my quad. Leaning back to elevate my knee, I swipe open Lila's message.

Lila: Hey Cade. Just wanted to say thanks again for today. Took me a while to find you in my phone – don't you think "Football God" is a bit much?

Laughing, I tap out a reply. Truth, I wasn't sure if she would message me at all, but this makes it more fun.

Me: What would you have saved me as?

Lila: California Cade?

Me: Ouch, I'm more than just a location.

Lila: ...Cocky Cade?

Me: Now I'm laughing.
Lila: Good luck at your first game.
Me: Come watch. You'll be impressed.
Lila: Cocky trumps California.
Lila: Maybe, I'll see.

4

LILA

A massive poster of David Beckham in his underwear greets me as I walk into my dorm room. Grinning at my new roommate's taste, I drop my bags on the bed that hasn't been claimed.

The girl I'm rooming with unpacked, adding picture frames to her desk and making her bed. Stooping to check out her photos, the door bangs open and I jump back from the desk, whirling around.

"Oh good, you're here," a southern drawl announces. Dropping her purse onto her bed, she walks over and pulls me into a hug. "I'm Kristen."

"Hey," I pat her back. "Lila."

"Oh, I know. I already checked with the Orientation people. I was wondering when you were going to show up. Anyway, welcome. Hope you don't mind; I picked the left side of the room."

"No, it's cool."

"Need help unpacking?"

"Uh—"

The door swings open again. "Oh my God. You're never

going to believe who I just saw. Cade freaking Wilkins. The football player. Talk about sexy." A tall, skinny guy leans against the doorjamb, one hand bracing himself from falling over, the other pushing his thick, green glasses up on his nose. "Men in California are too freaking yummy. That's why I'll never leave."

Kristen rolls her eyes. "Sam, this is Lila."

"You made it!" Sam strides over, grasps my shoulders, and kisses both of my cheeks. "Kris was starting to worry." He flops down on her bed, kicking off his flip-flops.

"Um, hi." I wave, unsure how to handle all this...familiarity.

"So, tell us your story." Sam sits up straighter, hunching forward.

"My story?"

"Yes. I need to know everything if we're going to be friends. And we are, obvi."

"Give her a minute, Sam. She just arrived," Kristen whispers.

"Perfect timing, Lila. I was thinking we could go down to Jose Maria's Cantina for margaritas." He checks his watch, his eyes narrowing. "Does nowish work? You can unpack afterward, right?"

"Uh," I stammer, taken aback by Sam's larger-than-life personality. My phone chimes with a text, and I pull it quickly from my back pocket.

Brandon: Hey. How's LA? When you can, give Mom a call. She's having a hard time ...

Ugh. My parent's messed-up issues follow me all the way across the country. Blocking out the message, I slip my phone into my back pocket. "Definitely. Let's get Mexican. I can go for a quesadilla with that margarita."

"Savage." Sam stands, throwing an arm around my shoulder. Steering me out of the dorm, he chatters the entire time like we're old friends.

Thirty minutes later, I'm tucked into a booth at Jose Maria's. Kristen sits across from me, dipping a nacho into guacamole while Sam flags down our waiter.

"Three more," he gestures to the empty glasses of habanero nectar from the gods we sucked down in minutes.

"So, like I was telling you guys, I saw Cade Wilkins while I was walking to your dorm."

"Who's he?" Kristen asks, biting into another nacho.

"Who's he? Seriously? He's like the hottest football player to ever grace Astor's field. And he's really good too. Girls fall all over him, teams try to recruit him, and professors are kind of obsessed with him. I forget how much you guys don't know since you don't go here."

"I met him at the airport in New York. He helped me find my dorm," I share, adding a ridiculous scoop of guac to my nacho.

"You talked to him?" Sam squeals, squeezing my arm.

"We split a taxi to campus."

"Oh my God. I'm so glad I decided to make you one of my besties for the semester."

Kristen snorts, raising one of the fresh margaritas in my direction. "To new friends. And a kick-ass semester with some California hotties."

Leaning back in my chair, I recall a similar pact I made a few weeks ago. "I'll drink to that."

"Same," Sam agrees, clinking his glass against mine and Kristen's.

ORIENTATION IS LAME: a bunch of doctors and school administrators blabbing about their expectations for the semester and nerdy looking students scribbling, eyes darting around to peek at their neighbor's notes. As soon as it's over, Kristen, Sam, and I beeline to the nearest restaurant to grab an early dinner.

"What's the deal, Sam? You should be tight with the other Astor students having spent the last three years taking classes with them. Why are you kicking it with the two of us newbies?" Kristen asks once we're seated at a table.

Sam fidgets in his chair, taking a long pull of his beer. "Did you guys notice Cliff Henderson?"

"Uh, yeah. It's hard not to notice Cliff Henderson," I admit. Cool, green eyes, disheveled brown hair, tall and muscular in all the right places, Cliff stood out in the crowd.

"We dated my sophomore year."

"And ..." I press.

"It didn't end well. Apparently, I'm too gay." He air quotes around gay, rolling his eyes. "And it made people uncomfortable."

"Cliff didn't tell the haters to fuck off?" I'm outraged by the small mindedness of my peers...in a medical program in California.

"No. He pretty much ghosted me."

"That's messed up. How can someone be too gay? That's like saying I'm too straight or Kristen is too human."

"It doesn't matter. It's in the past." Sam flicks his wrist dismissively but red patches form on his cheeks and he averts his gaze. "Anyway, after that, I was the outcast of the pre-med group."

Kristen rests her hand on top of Sam's. "I'm sorry, Sam. That sucks."

"Hard," I add.

Sam snorts, cracking a smile. "Yeah, it really did. But

now, eh, now I'm part of the Three Amigos…" his finger circles around our little group "…so it's not so bad."

"Gah! Don't go into stand-up comedy." I laugh anyway at his awful joke, picking up my sangria.

"I'd never cut it," he agrees. "Besides, my parents would kill me with how much they're shelling out for medical school."

"What programs are you applying to?" Kristen asks us.

"North Carolina, Cornell, Stanford for my reach." Sam shrugs. "You?" he looks at me.

"Uh, I'm not sure yet."

"Did you start your MCAT prep?" he frowns.

"Nope."

"Girl, you better get on that," Kristen advises.

"Have you guys?" I ask, not surprised when they both nod. "Damn."

"What's the holdup? Everyone I know has been application prepping for the last year."

"I haven't really thought about it."

"Say what?" Sam asks, incredulous. "Do you even want to go to medical school?" he jokes but when it falls flat in the space between us, his laughter dies. "Do you?" he peers at me, a line forming in between his eyebrows.

Taking a large gulp of sangria, I meet the confused expressions of my new friends. "I'm not sure. I mean, my grades are really good and I know I'll have solid recommendation letters but…"

"Then why are you here?" Kristen asks.

"My dad." I tell them the truth, the one I rarely share because it sounds so stupid when I say it aloud. Who lets their parents dictate their future like this?

"Is he a hardass?" Sam guesses.

"Kind of. It sounds so lame, right? Like, why do I need

his approval so badly? Will he give me a gold star if I have Dr. before my name?"

"Nah, we all have crap we deal with because of our parents' hang-ups. Don't stress it. See how the internship goes and if you like it, apply for med school. If not, at least you figured it out before getting into serious student loan debt."

Sam's words lessen the weight that hangs over my head every time I think about medical school, the MCATs, applications. He's right, testing out the internship before making a decision is a practical approach to my future.

"No one works in the field of their undergrad degree anyway," Kristen adds, her point reassuring

"You guys are making me feel way less like a failure."

"That's what friends do." Sam waves a hand as if it's obvious and I relax, relieved that I already have two real friends here.

GETTING BACK into the academic grind is jarring. Just because I'm good at school doesn't mean I like it. Halfway through the week, I take a moment to relax outside and enjoy the solitude of the evening. Tucking my legs underneath me on a campus bench, I close my eyes, letting my mind wander.

The shrill ring of my phone interrupts the quiet as Brandon's face lights up the screen.

"Hey."

"Hi, Li. How was orientation?"

"So lame. How are you?"

"Busy. So, you like the program?"

"I guess. I mean it's only been a few days."

"But...?" my brother prods.

Sighing, I try to align my thoughts so they sound coherent when they fall from my mouth.

"Lila? Is everything okay?"

"What do you think if I take a year off before applying to medical school?" I feel him out. There's no need to admit that I may not apply at all since I haven't made any concrete decisions.

"Why would you delay the inevitable? This isn't some weird hippie thing you want to do, is it? Like you're going to travel to an ashram in India for a year and find yourself? Or go backpacking across Australia with Emma?"

"No. I don't have a plan yet for what I want to do next year."

"Then why not just start medical school?"

"I don't know."

"It's tough to get back into the student mode once you've had a taste of the real world." This I've heard before. Mainly from my dad.

And I so don't want to take advice from Dad any longer.

"Maybe."

"So what gives?" he asks.

"I just, I don't know if I want to do it."

He whistles, the sound low. "Like at all?"

"Yeah."

"Did you talk to Dad?"

"I'm talking to you. What do you think?"

"I'm trying to figure out where this is coming from. A few weeks ago you seemed excited about this program. Did something happen at Astor?"

"No, nothing happened. And it's not just one thing, it's been a long time coming. I never questioned it because I'm good at the science courses and don't hate the labs like most people who drop out of the program."

Brandon snorts, "Don't tell people that. You'll have no friends."

"I know! But now that I'm here, in this program, I just don't... I don't really care. And sure, I know I *can* do it, but I don't really *want* to do it. Becoming a doctor isn't one of those things you change your mind about a few years down the road. You've got to be committed and I don't feel... anything really. No passion, no excitement, nothing. Aren't you supposed to be excited about your career?"

He's silent for a few minutes. Finally, he blows out a deep breath. "Yeah, Li. You are. I get it, trust me, I do. I felt the same way when I told Dad about law school instead of med school. I didn't have your grades though, so he gave me a bunch of BS about not being able to cut it anyway. Which I guess was a relief. Better he thinks I can't do it than I don't want to." Bran's voice is tinged with bitterness.

"What do you think I should do?"

"I think you better have a plan that doesn't include an ashram or a backpack when you tell Dad."

Laughter bubbles inside of me followed by relief when I realize Brandon is on my side. "Yeah, he would lose it if I told him I was going to do some farming co-op in Argentina."

Brandon snickers, "Join the Peace Corps."

"Volunteer at an orphanage."

We're cracking up in earnest now.

"Dad sucks sometimes."

"Totally," I agree. "How's Mom?"

"She's Mom."

"How bad?"

"Nothing for you to worry about."

"How bad?" I repeat.

"She's not in a great place. Dad is taking Brenda on a Caribbean cruise."

"Well, they are divorced now." I point out, irritated that I still rush to my dad's defense at all. About anything.

"Yeah, but you know how she feels about Brenda."

"I know." Mom can't stand her. Brenda was the quintessential other woman. She was Dad's colleague, who sent Bran and me birthday cards and chatted Mom up like old friends at the annual company picnic and Christmas party. But it's not like Mom didn't know about Dad's affair. Or, affairs. "But Mom's okay?"

"She's spending some time with Aunt Lori. I think she's depressed, but not suicidal if that's what you're thinking."

It is what I'm thinking but I don't voice my concern. No one wants to admit that they think their mother is so depressed, so broken, so lost that she would consider taking her own life. My chest squeezes and I rub the space above my breastbone, trying to alleviate the pressure. Just thinking about my mom hurts and as much as I know I should check up on her, things between us are always strained.

"Li? You okay?" Bran's tone is gentle, causing more emotion to build in my chest, travel up the column of my throat.

"Sure," I say, but the threat of tears is evident in my voice as my nose burns and the space behind my eyes stings.

"You don't have to be a tough guy about it. If you want to cry, cry. If you're pissed, be pissed. Do whatever you need to do, Li. This is a shitty situation and you're far away."

My big brother's concern causes the tears to bubble over. Several beats of silence pass as I try to control my emotions, halt my tears. My skin feels too tight, stretched, as hot tears slide down my cheeks, and I hold the phone away from my face so my brother won't hear.

"So are you," I challenge, hardening my tone.

"I've been living in Seattle for months. You've been in California for less than a week. You okay?"

"I'm fine." The shakiness in my voice betrays me.

"Lila."

"I'm okay." I take a deep breath. "Really. I need to start handling things on my own."

"Are you sure?"

"Yes."

"If you need anything, you call me, alright? I promise we're all going to get through this. Dad's life is his own. We can help Mom deal with everything the best that we can. And you and I, we'll be fine."

"I know."

"Hang in there, Li. Love you."

"Love you too. 'Bye."

Hanging up the phone, the quiet I was enjoying minutes ago now irritates me. Dark thoughts swirl in my mind, rubbing my emotional wounds raw, exposing my weakness to anyone who passes by. The uncertainty of my family's future grips me like a vise, threatening to choke me as a sob rises in my throat.

Dad is taking Brenda on vacation. What's next? Probably moving in together. Right now, he's living in the city apartment. Does he live there alone? Or does she already live with him?

An uncontrollable sob wells in my throat and before I can swallow it down, it escapes. Sitting on the bench, in the quiet of my new home, I sob hot tears, letting them track my cheeks and fall onto my knees. Gah! Why do I still react like this? My parents divorced a year ago, I should be over it by now.

Letting my tears fall is surprisingly cathartic, a release. I sit on the bench for a long time, until my racing heart slows, my thoughts quiet, and acceptance trumps the wild, over-whelming feelings from earlier.

Lifting the bottom of my tank top, I bury my face in my palms. My shirt absorbs the wetness from my skin. The balmy breeze soothes me, calming my erratic emotions.

My phone chimes and I groan, knowing it's Brandon checking up on me. But when I glance at the message, my heartrate accelerates. This time for an entirely different reason. A much better one.

Football God: Hey Lovely Lila. You busy tonight? Wanna grab an Italian ice?

Rolling my eyes at his moniker for me, the old hurts flaring to life inside are tempered by Cade's message.

Me: Lovely Lila?

Football God: Beats Lonely Lila doesn't it?

Snorting, I wipe the back of my hand across my cheek.

Me: Lonely may be more accurate. Warning: I'm not looking too lovely at the moment.

Football God: You okay?

Me: Yes, you have impeccable timing.

Football God: I'm taking that at face value because I'm picking you up in ten minutes.

Ten minutes? Ducking into the nearest building, I beeline to the bathroom. Splotchy cheeks and red-rimmed eyes greet me in the mirror. Damn it. Washing my face with cold water, I pat it dry with the rough, brown paper towels, wincing at my reflection. This would happen to me. The Football God himself asks me to hang out and I look like … this.

FML.

A million times over.

5

CADE

"What's wrong?" Every protective cell in my being flares to life when Lila climbs into my truck, her eyes red and her nose puffy. "Is someone bothering you?"

She chuckles, the sound lightening the weight sitting in the center of my chest. "Nothing like that. I'm being dramatic."

Raising my eyebrows, I take in her simple tank top and cut-off shorts, her arms and legs sun-kissed, her face devoid of makeup. She's not rocking heels and a miniskirt, stinking up my truck with a million hair products and body lotions. She is the opposite of most girls I know. She rocks a cardigan; there's nothing dramatic about that. "I don't believe you."

"Okay, fine. I'm one-hundred percent right for feeling everything I do and everyone else is wrong." She clicks in her seatbelt, quirking an eyebrow at me.

"There's the confidence I was waiting for." Pulling out of the parking lot, I turn onto the main road and reach over to squeeze her knee. "For real, what's going on?"

She sighs, her fingers plucking at mine. "A lot is going on

at home and I guess, I got overwhelmed. Lonely Lila needs a distraction."

Glancing over at her, she wrinkles her nose, and her expression is so adorable I want to scoop her up and hug her until all the sadness she's carrying around leaks out.

"I'm pretty good at providing distractions, lovely." Watching her for another beat, I search her face for a sign that something else is causing her distress. "You sure you don't want to talk about it?"

She shakes her head.

"Okay. Then tell me about your week. Are you all settled in?"

"Yeah, so far so good. I lucked out with my roommate, Kristen. She's pretty awesome, from Texas, and after meeting all the other girls in the program, I'm relieved we're paired together. We made friends with a guy named Sam, and the three of us just clicked. It's been a pretty easy transition with the two of them."

"How's the internship?"

"Ugh, it's fine."

"You don't like it?"

"It's okay. The people are nice and the program is really competitive so …"

I wait for her to continue.

"Are you excited for your first game?" She changes the subject.

Eyeing her, she meets my gaze expectantly, her body angled toward mine. Clearing my throat, I answer her question even though I've got several of my own. "Yeah. Arizona is a tough team, so it will be a good opener. Hopefully, we'll have a big win and set some momentum for the season."

"Is it weird that it's your last season?"

"Yes. My whole life, this has been the goal, to play

Division I football. Football has been my one constant, the thing that defines me. Now that it's almost over, it's kind of like, what next? I never thought about where I'd go from here because it never seemed like it was going to end, ya know?"

"Are you planning to go pro?"

"Yeah, well, that's everyone's dream, isn't it? We'll see what's in the cards for me. I'd love a shot, but I don't want to bank on that happening. One injury and it's all over."

"What do you want to do if you don't play football?"

"I have no idea." I shrug, pulling at the back of my neck. Damn, this girl is hitting me with the tough questions already. "I wish I was more like you, already decided on a career path. You can't go wrong with medicine."

"I guess."

Flipping on my blinker, I turn into the parking lot for Paolo's Italian Ice. "This is the best Italian ice you'll ever have."

"Hope you can back that claim up, Cade. I lived in New York; you're making a bold statement."

"Yeah, I know, babe. But I'm from Jersey so I'm pretty confident."

"We'll see." She unclicks her seatbelt and bends to retrieve her purse. By the time she straightens, I'm opening the car door for her.

"Thank you, kind sir." Lila grins, her eyes gaining some of that dazzle back. I dip into a small bow and she laughs, the tightness leaving her face as she starts to relax.

We walk into Paolo's and wait in line, reading the list of flavors.

"What's your favorite, Cade?"

"Lemon."

"Oh my God, you're so boring!"

"It may be basic, but it's a classic. What's yours? Don't say something dumb like bubble gum."

"Cherry."

"Because that's so much more original than lemon. They are the two most generic flavors. Except your whole mouth will turn red."

"Still worth it."

Ordering us two Italian ices, we head outside to an old picnic table on the side of the building. Lila sits on the bench, her elbows resting on top of the table. I straddle the bench next to her, facing her directly.

"Oh wow, this is amazing," she moans, taking her first taste of the ice.

"Told you."

"At least now I know you're honest. Is my tongue red?" she sticks out her bright red tongue.

"Your whole mouth is red. Teeth included."

"Damn," she murmurs, tucking back into her ice.

"It's a good look for you. It will pair nicely with your cardigan."

Dropping her head back, she laughs, wiping at the corners of her eyes. "Got jokes, do you, Cocky?"

"Just being honest with you, Lovely."

"Okay, real talk, then. What're you doing hanging with me, the new girl, when I know for a fact that your house is having a party tonight."

"How do you know that?"

"I have exactly two friends and they both mentioned it. If you hadn't invited me for Italian ice I may have been disappointed that you didn't invite me to your party."

"Is that right?" My mouth splits into a smirk. Leaning forward, I crowd her, breathe in her scent, coconut and summertime. Flyaway strands of her silky hair tickle my chin.

She nods, her eyes flaring with heat. But she doesn't look away, instead, she lifts her chin and asks again, "So, why'd you message me?"

"You're unlike any of the girls I know."

"Shiny new toy?" she guesses, her tone barbed with a hardness that scrapes at my skin.

"Never a toy. Come on, you've got too much confidence to reduce yourself to that." I cluck my tongue, disappointed.

"You're right." She lifts her chin even higher, her eyes boring into mine, searching for...what?

"I wanted to see you." The confession falls from my mouth on a whisper.

"Who's lonely now?" she grins.

"Who's acting cocky?" I taunt.

"I'm glad you messaged." Her gaze dips for a moment, staring at my chin, moisture collects in the corners of her eyes, some of her dazzle dimming.

Reaching out, I tug her closer, settle her between my thighs, and drop my chin to the top of her head. I hate not being able to read her eyes but I have a feeling she'll talk more if I'm not staring at her.

"Tell me what's going on. Who made you cry?" I trail my fingers up the lengths of her arms, fascinated by the goose-bumps that appear in the wake of my touch.

"You sure you're ready for my brand of crazy?"

"You're not going to scare me off that easily, Lovely. I once had a girl try to hit me with her car."

She snorts, a bubble of laughter escaping her nose. "What'd you do to piss her off?"

"Why do you assume it's my fault?"

"Isn't that the way of things? It's usually the man who fucks up."

Did I misread this? Is she upset about some dick from back home? An ex-boyfriend? Or worse, a current boyfriend?

She must feel me stiffen behind her because she snuggles closer into my embrace. "My dad made me cry. My parents, they got divorced last year. But still, everything is drama with them. My brother called a little bit before you messaged to tell me that my dad is going on vacation with his girlfriend, aka the woman he cheated on my mom with. Obviously, my mom isn't dealing with it very well. Anyway, I ... I don't know. It all hit me harder being so far away..." She trails off, shrugging her shoulders.

Is it messed up that I'm relieved she's upset about her family and not a guy?

Yeah, it is. And, not at all what I was expecting.

Her shoulders sag with her confession and she drops her head forward. Over her shoulder, I watch as she picks at the paper of her ice cup.

"Damn, Lovely. That's...a lot." Hugging her closer, I drop my chin to her shoulder.

"Way too heavy for a first date," she quips, turning her head toward me before she freezes, as if realizing her slip. "I mean, you know—"

Wrapping my hand around her loose waves, I move her hair to the side and run my nose over the shell of her ear. "You're being real, Lila, and I want to know the real you."

She rolls the back of her head against my chest and I pluck her ice up off the picnic bench and place it back in her hands. "Your ice is melting."

"Thanks, Cade," she whispers, shifting out of my embrace and eating some of her cherry ice.

"I'm really sorry about your parents. That's a tough one, especially being so far from home."

"Yeah. It's tough knowing my mom is by herself. Not that

I lived at home but I was a lot closer in Philly. And my brother relocated to Seattle a few months ago so it's been tough on her." She shrugs sheepishly. "Do you have any siblings?"

"I did." The words stick in my throat. I hate telling anyone about Jared, hate talking about it at all. But after she was so candid with me, I want to be real with her. "Jared. He passed away last year in Iraq. He was a Marine."

"Cade, I'm so sorry. I wouldn't have asked if…" she turns toward me, placing a hand on my forearm.

"It's a fair question."

"You wear his dog tags."

"How do you know that?"

"I saw them at the airport. At first, I thought maybe you were military."

"Nah. Just my brother."

"Were you close?"

"He taught me pretty much everything I know."

Her face falls, anguish striking her features. "I can't even imagine. I'm sorry."

"Thank you." My voice sounds gruff, closed off, even to me. "Want to go for a drive?" I change the subject.

"Sure." She stands quickly. Too quickly.

Tossing our paper cups into the garbage can, I follow her back to my truck. The air between us is thick, tense. Gone is the chatter about smiling e's. We've revealed too much, too soon.

When I start the engine, she leans over and fiddles with the radio, settling on a random station. "Jingle Bell Rock" comes on, and she snorts, glancing at me in her peripheral vision. Closing her eyes, she sings, loudly and off-key.

What the hell?

"Don't leave me hanging, Cade. I know you know this song."

Cardigan girl, lonely and lovely Lila, is tripping me up. Who can get me to discuss my brother one minute and make me want to sing Christmas tunes the next?

"I don't hear you," she taunts.

Shaking my head, the lyrics float in my mind like it's the middle of December and I join in. Our voices meld together, the awkwardness evaporating.

"What station is this?"

"How would I know?" she shrugs. "But Christmas is my favorite. I love December and winter and snow. Plus, the presents and Christmas cookies and mistletoe. Everything seems so magical that time of year."

"You're crazy. No one from Jersey likes winter and snow."

"What's your favorite Christmas song, Cade?"

"Dominic the Donkey."

"Stop!" She smacks her hand against my arm and howls with laughter.

Drinking in her open expression, the graceful column of her neck, the bright dazzle of her eyes, I think I fall a little bit in love with her. Uninhibited, natural, and carefree, Lila's enthusiasm overshadows the heaviness of our previous conversation.

There are no ulterior motives with her. She doesn't care that I play football and may get drafted. She isn't trying to be someone she's not or angling to impress me. Her honesty, her confidence, and her humor are so much sexier than the fake tits and sexual innuendos girls usually throw my way.

We drive aimlessly, singing along with the radio, and talking. Lila shares wild tales of her best friends—Mia, Emma, and Maura—and their college shenanigans. I have her cracking up with the best pranks my football team has carried out over the past few seasons.

Too soon, I'm pulling in front of her dorm, parking the truck.

She unclicks her seatbelt and turns the radio down. "Thank you for tonight, Cocky. Truly."

Tucking a strand of hair behind her ear, my fingers linger, trail down the column of her neck. I can't stop touching her, wanting to be close to her, hanging onto her every word. With each passing moment, I bend my rules even more, distorting them. "Yeah, well, you hurt my ego a bit. No one's actually cried hanging out with me before."

"Glad I could be a first for you."

My palms slide over her shoulders, her warmth seeping into my skin. "We'll have to do it again sometime soon. You know, make sure the crying was a fluke."

Biting her lower lip, her eyes latch onto mine, serious and searching. I want to tug her into my lap, kiss her senseless, and catch every single gasp that falls from her mouth. But I force myself to stay still, let her command this exchange, decide what, if anything, unfolds between us.

A full minute passes, the air in my truck thickening with the sound of our breathing, the weight of unsaid words. Leaning over the center console, her palms cup my cheeks, their softness rubbing against the coarse stubble along my jaw. The tiniest inhale of breath ripples between us, skating over my skin. Inside, I'm practically shaking with anticipation, my blood humming with need for Lila. Her touch is like a gateway drug and I crave more. I want everything she's willing to give.

The corners of her mouth lift slowly, her blue eyes shimmering as they hold mine. Her gaze drops to my lips and then she's shifting, sliding onto her knees, leaning over the center console, and finally, pressing her lips against mine.

My mouth parts for her automatically, partially in desperation and partially in gratitude. Deepening our kiss, I slant my mouth over hers, tracing the seam of her lips with my tongue. Her lips part on a sigh and our tongues meet, dancing around each other, slow and sweet.

But then her palms slide up, gripping at my hair and my restraint snaps as my need for her spirals. Groaning, I pull her over the center console until she's settled in my lap, straddling me. Her fingers hook around the back of my neck, her breasts pushed against my chest, the soft swell tormenting me.

My hand splays across her back, my pinky digging into the dip above her ass while my thumb skirts the thick band of her bra. And hell, I want to snap it open, pull her tank top over her head, and recline my seat all the way back until she's flush against me.

But I can't. Won't. Because it's too much, too soon. All of this is more than I anticipated. More than I can wrap my head around.

Ripping my lips away from hers, I grip her shoulders and add some space between us. We're both panting, trying to catch our breath. Dropping my forehead to hers, my palms slide down to curl around her elbows.

"Cade, I –"

"Fuck, I want you, Lovely." The admission drops from my lips on a groan, surprising both of us.

A grin twitches across Lila's lips, her eyes snapping up to mine. "Then what's wrong?" she whispers the words and I hear the unease, the fear of rejection, in them.

"Nothing's wrong, babe. It's all right, all good. I just, damn, I don't do commitment and relationships and —"

"Monogamy?"

"That too." My palms glide up and down her arms. The desperation I feel to touch her unnerves me. It's too intense. Everything is too damn raw, too real. "But I like you, Lovely. And I'm not messing this up after one time kicking it with you. Feel me?"

She nods, her eyes wide. Brushing a sweet, sensual kiss against my mouth, she straightens her tank top and crawls back to the passenger side of my truck. "Good luck on Saturday, Cocky." She glances at me over her shoulder, her eyes smoldering, her lips beestung and slick from my kiss.

Hopping out of my truck, she offers a small wave, before disappearing into her dorm.

I sit in my truck and drop my head to the steering wheel.

The taste of cherry ice lingers on my lips.

6

LILA

S eptember 9
11:42 PM
Group Text: Me, Emma, Mia, Maura
Me: I kissed a football god. And I'm smitten.
Emma: Shut up.
Maura: Already?
Mia: Where?
Emma: Details, bitch.
Me: I met him at the airport on my flight to LA. We both got bumped.
Emma: And???
Me: We went for Italian ice and I kissed him.
Maura: Hold up, you kissed him or he kissed you?
Me: ...both
Emma: Well played, my friend, well played.
Mia: Are you going to see him again?
Me: I really hope so. He's...
Maura: Are you speechless?
Me: (Blushing emoji)
Emma: (Praising hands emoji x 10)

Mia: Wow. I'm impressed, Lila.

Emma: Bow to the Queen. (crown emoji x 3)

Me: What's going on by you guys?

Emma: My internship starts Monday. (puke face emoji)

Mia: You're going to do great, Em. I may have met an Italiano.

Maura: May have? You either met one or didn't.

Mia: I met one. I just, I don't know what to make of him yet.

Emma: Fair... please keep us informed of all updates. Maura??

Maura: As if any of you are surprised that nothing is going on in my life. I'm waking up for practice at the crack of dawn.

Emma: That's gross.

Me: I miss you girls.

Maura: Tell me about it.

Mia: Me too! I have to get ready for class now. Google hangout soon?

Emma: Duh. I want to hear about the Italiano! How's your Italian coming along? If he whispered sweet nothings in your ear, would you understand him?

Mia: Ciao amiche.

Maura: Goodnight guys.

Emma: Lila, send me photos of your football god.

Me: Let me know how Monday goes.

Emma: (purple hearts x 5)

Locking the screen of my phone, I slip it onto my nightstand. Kristen snores softly in her bed, already asleep when I returned home from hanging out with Cade. I'm sure her and Sam, well, mostly Sam, are going to lose it when I tell them tomorrow.

Turning off my bedside lamp, I close my eyes, hoping

sleep comes quickly. Tomorrow promises long hours of dressing wounds and changing bedpans. Just think, people actually want to become doctors...

THE REST of the week passes quickly with a few general messages from Cade asking about my internship and one fantastic Instagram photo of Mia tossing coins into the Trevi Fountain.

Finally, Saturday arrives and with it, the weekend. But more importantly, game day. Sam scored the Three Amigos tickets to the game and insisted that Kristen and I attend, tail-gating included.

"You have to go to his game," he tells me, flipping through the clothes hanging in my closet. "It will give you something to talk about the next time you kiss, I mean, see each other."

"I don't even know when I'll see him again. I don't want to seem like I'm stalking him."

"Be real. There will be over 70,000 people at the game today. Everyone goes. You would be a weirdo for not going." He pauses to inspect the graphic on one of my shirts. "You really have no cool clothes."

"Thanks, fashionista."

Kristen returns to our dorm room, the door banging as it smacks against the wall.

"Look what I got!" she squeals, holding up a bag from the campus bookstore.

"More notebooks?" Sam guesses.

"Stickers and color pens?" I chime in.

"No." Kristen flips over the bag, the contents pouring onto her bed. "Game day gear." She holds up a handful of tank tops, baseball caps, and other gold and plum accessories.

"You're a savior." Sam exits my closet and drops dramatically onto my bed. "You seriously have nothing that is gold or plum. No Astor colors at all," he tsks at me. "And don't even get me started on your graphic tee collection."

"Well, now she does," Kristen holds up a cute off-the-shoulder white top that says Astor across the front in Astor plum outlined by Astor gold. Mustang colors.

"Love this!" Sam grabs the shirt. "Wear it with tight jeans … wait," he raises his watch to his lips. "Siri, what is the temperature outside?" His eyebrows disappear into his hairline. "Never mind, it's too hot. Wear denim shorts, but not those cut-off ones you wore yesterday, the ones with the cuffs on the bottom. And flip-flops. Or boots with the laces open and untied. Yes, I like that look." He hands the shirt to me before spinning on his heel. "What are you wearing?" he asks Kristen pointedly. "I have a reputation to maintain, you know?"

Kristen holds up a plum tank, Mustangs running up the left side in gold.

"Perfect." Sam nods in approval. "Okay." He claps. "You girls get dressed and hot. I'll meet you in thirty so we can start tailgating. Victory is ours!" He fist pumps, yelling a war cry.

Kristen makes a fist pump and echoes Sam's chant. Peeling off her shirt, she tugs the tank top over her head. "Today is going to be awesome. I haven't been to a real football game in ages. My school has hockey." She grimaces as her face emerges from the tank top.

"You know, I've never done the football game and tailgate scene. My college is all about basketball."

"Oh girl, you better get ready for it. There's nothing like a football tailgate. Especially in the South or at a school like Astor, D-1 and top ranking."

Entering my closet, I pull my phone out of my back pocket to change. Scanning the front screen, my heart leaps into my throat as I see a message from Cade. Then it shrivels in response to a message from my dad.

Football God: Morning Lovely, you best be all dressed up in your finest plum and gold.

Me: You would hardly recognize me. I look like I ransacked the bookstore.

Dad: Lila, please stop ignoring my calls. We need to talk. Call me today.

Meh. Does that warrant a reply? My finger hovers over the delete button as I weigh my options. Nah. I press delete. I don't want to talk to my dad and have him ruin my idea of my family, listening to him crush the happy memories I have left with three simple words.

I moved on.

Although Brandon already filled me in on the details, I'm not ready to hear it from Dad. Maybe I'm acting childish but like every kid of divorced parents that I know, I still awkwardly hold out hope that they will get back together, despite all of their issues. That Dad will change his ways. That Mom will force him to be more open and honest. That things will work out like they did in that Lindsay Lohan movie from the nineties, *The Parent Trap*.

And if that doesn't happen, then it's just easier to dwell in denial. Pretend that Mom is coping. Pretend that Dad is sympathetic and understanding to her feelings. Pretend to have all the appropriate reactions of a twenty-one-year-old dealing with her parents' divorce. Because really, what's the alternative?

Football God: You coming to cheer me on?

Me: I'll be there, foam finger in hand. What's your number?

Football God: 33. Gotta love the foam fingers. Have you nabbed a beer cozie yet? Keep an eye out for those.

Me: I'll need one for my cup of tequila.

Football God: Don't forget the limes.

Me: Packing salt in my purse.

Football God: Have fun today.

Me: Good luck.

Changing into the denim shorts Sam advised, a shimmy of excitement works down my spine. Is it weird that I want to cheer for Cade, even if I'm one among seventy-thousand?

I'm scrunching my fingers through my roots for more volume when my phone chimes. My heart accelerates and I roll my eyes at myself. Giddy much?

Football God: Don't need it. I have a feeling you'll be my good luck charm.

Heat spreads across my neck and cheeks at his words. His good luck charm? He never said anything about our Italian ice being a date or not but there's definitely something more than just the physical chemistry between us. And that part is fire. Blazing, wild, all-consuming, Cade makes me feel too many things to care whether or not I end up burned.

When I turn around, Kristen is before me, holding out a bottle of perfume. "Here," she says, spritzing onto my wrist and neck. "You're cheesing too hard."

"Cade messaged." I hold up my phone.

"Seriously?" she squeals, her excitement matching my own. "What did he say?"

I drop my phone into her open hand and she scrolls through our exchange.

"OMG. He likes you, Lila. For real."

"I don't know. I totally jumped the gun and kissed him before he could make a move."

"I'm sure he loved being caught off guard. Guys like a girl they can't automatically read. Let's do a quick shot before we meet Sam." She rummages through her closet for a bottle of tequila. "To football, tailgates, and number thirty-three." She raises the bottle in my direction and takes a swig.

When she passes it to me, I raise it back in her direction. "Victory is ours." I hold up my fist and swallow a mouthful. The tequila burns my throat without a chaser to follow it, and I screw my eyes shut. "Damn, Kristen, this is strong."

"I'm a Texan."

"Clearly. Let's go."

SAM WAS RIGHT. I've never experienced anything like this in my life. The quad is teeming with tents and grills and kegs. Waves of people decked out in plum and gold overwhelm the space, blotting out all other colors. Reggaetón music blares and students dance in large circles, their bodies swaying, their red Solo cups brimming with beer.

McShain University is tiny compared to Astor. We have an awesome basketball team, and rowing of course, but that's about all we boast when it comes to sports. There's no stadium that holds over 70,000 cheering fans. There aren't any mass tailgates with tents and kegs. Astor is the real-life version of the college campuses featured in every teen movie.

The scent of fresh-cut grass and cheeseburgers overwhelm me, transporting me to Brandon's high school football games. Mom, Dad, and I always arrived early to host a tailgate. Dad behind the grill, his tongs flashing as he turned chicken wings and flipped burgers. Mom's pleasantries as she served pieces of pie and refilled massive bowls with potato chips and Doritos. Closing my eyes and breathing in deeply, I revel in the nostalgia of perfect autumn days with my perfect family.

Before we shattered.

"What do you think? Crazy, am I right?" Sam nudges me.

"Totally."

"Okay, let's meet some people over at the fountain and then we can walk around. I'll introduce you to some friends."

Kristen and I follow Sam wordlessly. Kristen's excitement is palpable, and I feel a rush of affection for my new friend who has made my first week in California an easy transition.

When we arrive at the huge circular fountain in the center of the quad, Sam's friends are milling about, sipping on beers and chomping on burgers.

"Hey, guys," Sam announces, waving his arm in front of Kristen and me. "These are my friends from the med program, Kristen and Lila. This is their first Astor game, so show them some love and fun."

A chorus of introductions ring out and I am lost in the sea of unfamiliar faces and new names.

Kristen clutches my elbow. "Don't leave me, okay?"

"No way. We're in this together."

Sam hands us each a red Solo cup of beer and places Mardi Gras beads around our necks. "To the Three Amigos."

"Victory is ours!"

7

CADE

G ame day. Season opener. My last first game.

When I wake in the morning, my muscles automatically tense with the excitement and anticipation for today. I love game day. I love the crowds, the endless expanse of plum and gold, the Mustang mascot, the marching band, the burgers and beer of tailgates. I live for the adrenaline rush of taking the field, the spring of grass underneath my cleats, the camaraderie and pep talks from the locker room.

My team.

My game.

Victory is ours.

Stretching slowly, I mentally assess each part of my body. My knee throbs, an ache radiating from just below my kneecap into the surrounding muscle. I massage it and make a mental note to ask the trainer to wrap it. Cracking my neck, I shake off sleep and sit on the edge of my bed to check my phone.

10:34AM.

What the hell? I never sleep in on game days. Or any days. Most mornings, I barely make it to 8AM. Blowing out a breath, I chalk it up to the stress of the past few weeks, our questionable ranking for this season, and the one-year memorial of Jared's passing.

Mama: Good luck today, Cade. Thinking of my number 33! I'll be watching. Dad and Uncle Ronnie are excited. Love you!

Me: Thanks, Mama. Love you.

Miers knocks on the door, pushing it open seconds later. "Yo, you up?"

"Barely." I grab a pair of athletic shorts off the floor and slip them on, standing up to pull the shorts in place.

"Well, get your ass in gear. Hendrix is at the stove fixin' us one hell of a game-day breakfast."

Hendrix is the renaissance man of our team. He's a phenomenal athlete, a legit friend, and he makes the best pancakes I've ever had. When I first moved into the football house, we had a cook come in daily to prepare our meals. Now, Edith comes every day except game day, when Hendrix takes over. It's become a tradition, with all the guys pitching in to create a game-day breakfast: eggs, omelets, whole-wheat pancakes, whole grain waffles, turkey bacon, fruit salad. It's the best start to a game day and helps build a team hype that lasts past kickoff.

"In that case, I'm up."

"Thought so." Miers grabs a T-shirt off the back of my desk chair and throws it at me. I tug it over my head.

"I'll be down in a few minutes."

"Okay." He closes my door.

My knee twinges, little spikes of pain traveling up into my quad. I massage it again and sit back on my bed until the pain subsides. Then I join my team for breakfast.

Entering the kitchen, Hendrix is at the stove, a dishtowel thrown over his left shoulder. He's sliding back and forth, dancing to the oldies' radio station he has blaring from portable speakers. He's barefoot, donning Astor athletic shorts and a white wife beater that is already splattered with bits of oil and egg. He snickers at me when I reach past him to grab a mug.

"Yo. You turn into Sleeping Beauty or what?" He nods toward the clock.

"Yeah. I don't know what happened."

A dishtowel snaps against my ass and I turn quickly. Gogs stands behind me, twirling the dishtowel. "Morning, princess. Get your twelve hours of beauty rest?"

"Fuck off."

Gogs breaks a bagel in half, tossing me a piece.

I catch it easily and dunk it into an open jar of peanut butter.

"Hey. Out of my kitchen. Don't eat too much. Breakfast will be ready in ten." Hendrix waves a hand toward the living room. "Ooh, this is my jam!" He sings as "Baby I Need Your Loving" by the Four Tops floods the kitchen.

"He's going to be an awesome grandfather," Darrell Hayes says, throwing an arm around my neck. "You ready for today?"

"Yeah. You?"

"Hell yeah. We got this. We start the season off with a bang, set the energy, build the buzz. This is our senior year. I'm not leaving that field a loser."

He's right. This is our senior year, our final chance to take Astor all the way to the Rose Bowl, and I don't want to have any regrets about my last season as an Astor player.

"Breakfast," Hendrix announces over the music.

The nine of us who live in the house swarm the kitchen. It will only be a matter of minutes before the rest of the guys show up. But everyone knows seniors get first dibs.

And today is my last first game.

THE STADIUM IS OVERWHELMING in the best way imaginable. Plum and gold assault my eyes at every turn. Girls cheer loudly, waving Mardi Gras beads and dancing in the stands. Guys paint their faces and chests, whooping and raising their fists in war cries. The "Victory is Ours" song booms and pulses over the crowd as Marty the Mustang dances on the sidelines, throwing rolled up T-shirts and foam footballs to fans. Our marching band plays the alma mater, cheerleaders perform basket tosses on the sidelines and 70,000 people whistle, shriek, and clap, bringing the stadium to life.

My heart quickens, my blood pulsing in my eardrums. Ducking back into the locker room, I clasp at Jared's dog tags underneath my shirt. Taking them off, I squeeze them in my palm, mentally reciting a prayer Dad taught Jared and me years ago, when we first started playing football.

I hang my head and think of my brother, his finesse on the football field, his natural ability to lead, his voice echoing through the cheers of the crowd whenever he came to my games.

This season is for him.

"Huddle up!" Coach's voice reverberates through the locker room.

My team gathers around, in various states of dress. Coach goes over some plays before we finish suiting up. The room quiets down with everyone lost in their own thoughts. For us seniors, the weight of today bears down on us.

"Wilkins!" Coach slaps a heavy hand on my shoulder. "You all set for today? I noticed you've been favoring that right knee. All straight?"

"Yes, sir."

"Then give 'em hell."

I nod once, a snap of my neck.

My team huddles up once more. Hendrix gives an emotional pep talk. The fans grow louder. The beat of my heart pumps in my head, the blood thrumming in my ears.

"See you out there." Miers bangs his fist against my shoulder.

The Astor Mustangs take the field and the stadium roars. Fans whistle and cheer, pom-poms shimmer, signs and banners flash and wave. Today is game day. Victory is ours.

BY THE FOURTH QUARTER, the night lights have been flipped on, and the breeze has picked up, cooling the rivulets of sweat behind my ears and down my neck. It's 32-28 Arizona and my limbs feel jittery, antsy, with the need to score a touchdown.

In my peripheral vision, I see the throngs of fans on their feet, note their open mouths which must be screaming. But out here, on the field, even the slam of bodies and the snap of the football are secondary to the quiet in my head.

Stay hungry. Stay focused.

The ref calls an Astor first-down. We're on the forty-yard line.

Taking a deep breath, I ignore the ache in my knee, the burn of my shoulder from where it connected with the field during a tackle in the second quarter. Clearing my head of all thoughts, of all noise, I zero in on this moment, this play.

Gilly snaps the ball to Johnson. He takes a few steps back and I cut to the far left, my legs pumping, my lungs burning, adrenaline skyrocketing. Johnson throws a clean, crisp pass, and I catch the ball, tucking it protectively under my arm. Running toward the end zone, my legs are on fire, pushing me, fueling me.

Twenty-yard line.

I'm flying, my gaze singularly focused on the end zone. I hear the thud of tackles around me as our fullbacks block any attempts by Arizona players to take me down.

Holding my breath in my lungs, I cross into the end zone.

"Hell yeah!" Miers grabs my helmet as Hayes and Hendrix smack my shoulders.

Grabbing water from the water station, Coach pulls me aside.

"You sure everything is okay with your right leg, thirty-three?"

"Yes, sir. It's just been a little sore."

"Okay. Well make sure you pop by to see the trainer." He taps my helmet with the palm of his hand.

Back in the game, only a minute passes before Arizona scores a touchdown, putting them in the lead and raising the stakes, piling on the pressure.

Stay hungry. Stay focused.

The words are a mantra and I cling to them, digging deeper when my body feels like it's crumbling.

With three minutes left on the clock, Johnson throws a beautiful pass directly to me. I catch the ball, cradle it against my chest, and take off. As each step pounds into the field, twinges of pain radiate around my right knee. Gritting my teeth, I block out the pain, keep my head down and my eyes glued to the end zone. When I leap across the line, I'm gasping for air, wincing in pain. But as the burn in my knee dissipates, my breathing returns to normal, and by the time my teammates swarm me, I'm able to joke with them.

Fish scores an extra point and we manage to sneak in a field goal with forty seconds remaining.

We win.

45-39 Astor. Mustangs. Plum and gold.

The stadium erupts as the fans go wild. Ear-splitting cheers rush me as I look up, allowing the noise to filter back into my consciousness. Everyone in the crowd is on their feet, the stands pulsing with energy, with intensity, with life. Waving signs, singing songs, high-fives and hugs. People from all backgrounds and ages and beliefs coming together to celebrate this moment, this game, this. It's fucking beautiful and as the high of the win wraps around me, my stress leaks away, and I'm left with overwhelming gratitude that I get to play this game with these guys.

When we're back in the locker room and the team is settling down, I grip Jared's dog tags.

"Thanks, man."

8

LILA

The mayhem that ensues after the Astor win is insane. Fans cheer and chant; the band plays loudly; the mascot does backflips up and down the sidelines. I've never experienced team and school spirit of this caliber before, and I love being caught up in it.

Kristen jumps up and down next to me, my arm flailing as it's clasped in her hands. Sam whistles, his hands clapping above his head. The fans closest to us pull us into hugs, their arms thrown around our shoulders, as if we all participated in securing this win. Together. Bewilderment floods my system and I drink in the scene, an incredulous bubble of laughter erupting from my throat. If this is what a first-game win looks and feels like, I can't imagine the pandemonium that would ensue if Astor wins the Rose Bowl.

As we descend the bleachers and make our way to the exit of the stadium, I tell Kristen and Sam that I'm planning to wait for Cade.

Kristen smiles as Sam makes kissing faces at me. I palm his face and push him away. "I'll see you later."

"We're going to try and get some food." Sam gestures to

a group of his friends. "Lila, message me later so we can reconnect."

"Sounds good."

Sam pulls Kristen to his group of friends and I make my way against the sway of bodies to wait near the locker rooms.

While I wait for Cade, I pull out my phone and open the Facebook app. Emma posted photos of her first Friday night in D.C. There's a group shot of a bunch of people posing in front of a bar, their eyes bright with liquor and the anticipation of being in a new city with new people. Emma cheeses hard, flashing the peace sign, as the hot guy next to her, tall with sandy hair curling in the heat, throws an arm around her shoulders. I give the photo a thumbs-up like and check my email, happy to see a new thread from Mia.

To: lila.avers@mcshain.edu,   emma.stanton@mcshain.edu, maura.rodriguez@mcshain.edu

From: amelia.petrella@mcshain.edu

Date: September 12

Subject: Roma é il mio cuore

Ciao amiche,

Roma is my heart; I am seriously in love with this city but missing all of you tons and tons. I wish you could come visit. Lila – did you go to Cade's game? I need details. Emma – loving your photos from D.C. Who is the tall guy with his arm around you in the group photo? Maura – how are practices going?

Here's what's happening here:

My host family is incredible. Paola and Gianluca have taken me and Lexi (the other study abroad student) in as their daughters (even though they're like thirty). Gianluca cooks the most amazing dinners every night. I'm practicing my Italian constantly and think if this keeps up, I could be fluent. Imagine? My mom would be so happy!

Classes are going well. There's a boy in my class, Peter, and we are paired together for a project. He's really nice and has been helpful as I settle in here. Also, the Italiano. I met Lorenzo my first day here and since then, I've run into him frequently. I think his family owns the restaurant I study at. Plus, Lexi and I eat there a lot for lunch and he always adds a sweet – cannoli, biscotti, tiramisu, etc. – for us to take home.

Off to class now but looking forward to your updates. Hope you're all having a great weekend! Please write back soon.

Un bacione,
Mia

Way to go, Mia! Two boys. Her email is comforting, a connection to the girls who have been my constants for the past three years. Even though I'm at Astor, living my best life, it seems like I'm not so far from my besties when we continue to share our experiences. It's only been one week and yet it's as if a whole new world has opened up for each of us.

9

CADE

E xiting the locker room on a wave of unprecedented energy, I stop short when I see her. Leaning against the side of the building, her blond tresses a halo around her face, she's mesmerizing. Lila scrolls through her phone, a smile flitting across her lips, an unexpected giggle dropping from her mouth.

As much as I hoped to see her, I didn't expect her to wait on me.

"Hey Lovely," I call out.

"Hey, superstar!" she looks up, her eyes dancing, as she drops her phone in her purse.

"What happened to Cocky?" I walk over to her, adjusting my duffle bag higher on my shoulder, ignoring the other girls who call out my name and number.

"When you play like that, you deserve to be cocky so I'm not going to give you a hard time about it." She grins.

"Thanks for waiting on me."

"Yeah, well, just your newest groupie. President of the Cade Wilkins fan club."

"Is that right?" I cut the distance between us.

She glides her palm along the side of her body. "You like my gear?"

"Love it. Love that you're here even more."

When I reach her side, I hook my fingers underneath her chin, tilting her face back. Her eyes are like glitter, sparkling with excitement. Leaning down, I brush my lips over hers, feeling her mouth curl into a smile before she kisses me back.

"That was an awesome game," she congratulates, breaking our embrace.

"The best start to a season. I'm relieved we managed to kick it off with a W." I toss an arm around her shoulders and steer her toward my truck. "Were you waiting for me long?"

"No, only about ten minutes. It took me longer to fight off all your other groupies. I was the last one standing."

"You got jokes." I pinch the tip of her nose, holding the truck door open for her. "Put your seatbelt on." I close the door before sliding behind the steering wheel and flipping the ignition. "You hungry?"

"A little. Not starving but up for a snack."

"Well, I'm starving. You want to grab a pizza and then head back to my house? We're having a blowout party which probably started minutes after we won."

"Sure. Can I invite Kristen and Sam?" she asks, her hands toying with the hem of her shirt.

"Invite anyone you want. It's probably insane already."

"Cool." She takes out her phone and sends a text before dropping her purse back by her feet. "Where to?"

"I know a place."

PIZZA WITH LILA IS EASY, lighthearted. There are no ulterior motives, no expectations, just chill conversation. She tells me

more about how she grew up, her family dynamics, her brother Brandon. It's obvious by how she talks about him that they're close. Like Jared and I were.

Listening to her stories, watching how animated she is, I'm hanging onto every word that leaves her mouth. It's a heady – yet frightening – realization. It's barely been a week since this girl taught me about Heineken's smiling e's and I'm already breaking my rules.

I never walk into a house, a party, with a girl on my arm. But with Lila, I want to. I want the guys on my team, and any other lurkers, to know that she's with me, that I'm laying claim to her.

And hell, I don't ever do shit like that. Never cared before if a girl I was hooking up with was seeing other dudes. As soon as I learned she was, I quit her. It never mattered one way or the other because a slew of other females were desperate to take her place.

But God help me if I witness another guy step to Lila.

Pulling up to my house after pizza, I park around the back where there is a small lot with designated parking spots. I'm thankful that mine is still empty. The house is already packed, music pulsing all the way outside, the windows vibrating from the loud beats. Several partygoers spill onto the porch, drinking from red Solo cups.

Every time I take a girl out, until Lovely that is, there were always these expectations that came along with it. Are we together? Are you going to introduce me to the team? What do you mean we're not exclusive?

Glancing over at Lila, she twists a gold bangle around her wrist, and tugs on the bottom of her shirt, causing the sleeve to slip lower on her shoulder. The stretch of smooth, tanned skin tempts me and I drop a kiss there. "You know that by us showing up together, everyone is going to assume we're dating. You okay with that?"

She rakes her teeth over her bottom lip as she considers my question. "I think so. But we're cool, me and you, right?"

"Of course."

"Because I'm not trying to do some serious relationship my senior year."

For real? I toss my head back and laugh, the sound surprising us both.

"What?" Lila asks, a grin splitting her lips.

"You're so refreshing, you know that?"

She shrugs, the bare skin of her shoulder snagging my attention once more.

"Lila, listen, I haven't been in a serious relationship, if you could even call it that, since high school. I never show up to parties with a girl. I kick it, keep things chill, casual. But something about you is different and that's not me feeding you some bullshit line. I like you, like kicking it with you. But, for real, I'm not trying to tangle up in something serious my senior year either."

She bites her bottom lip again, her eyes flashing as she peers up at me from under long, long eyelashes. "So, we're cool?"

"We're more than cool. But if you don't want to deal with everything people are going to say if you walk through that door with me, I get it."

"Nah. I don't care what anyone says. You were my first friend here, before I even got here." She gestures outside. "Besides, people are going to talk regardless."

"Come on." I tilt my head toward the house. We exit my truck and I lace my fingers with hers, giving her hand a gentle squeeze. "Parties here can sometimes be overwhelming. If

any of this," I nod in the direction of the house, the party, "becomes too much, just let me know."

"Just make sure the beer is Heineken," she jokes, dropping my hand.

As we approach the house, a few guys whistle, two girls I once hooked up with stare, and people I don't know at all whisper behind their hands. It's only going to intensify once we cross the threshold but I don't care. In fact, I welcome it. I want everyone to know that Lila's here with me, and thereby off-limits. I may not be into a serious commitment but I also don't want her hooking up with other guys. Selfish? Yes. Messed-up? Maybe. But I don't care because I like this girl too much, more than just a hook-up, but as a person.

"You ready to hold the top spot for this week's campus gossip?" We walk up the four steps to the front door.

"Don't worry about me, Cocky. I'm only here for the semester. As soon as people start to care, I'll be gone." She says and I hate that her words cause a pang in my chest. She's right, she is only here for four months but the realization bothers me. More than it should.

Pushing the door open, we step inside. As soon as people see me, a roar erupts: cheering, clapping, whistling. I duck my head, embarrassed. Really, every win is a team win. Shaking off the applause, I pull Lila into the kitchen to grab some beers.

Within moments, the looks, the stares, the whispers begin.

"Who is she?"

"I've never seen her before."

"Is Cade with someone?"

"That won't last long."

I ignore the comments without even blinking. I can only hope that Lila is doing the same and isn't affected by the sneers from these random girls.

"Yo, dude." Miers calls out, holding out two red Solo cups fresh with beer from the keg. "Shit's almost tapped. Better get a beer while you can." He passes me a beer and hands the other to Lila. "Hey. I'm Miers."

Lila takes the cup. "Lila."

"Good to meet you."

"Same. Good game. You guys killed it."

"Thanks. What did you crazy kids get into tonight?"

"Pizza. It was pretty wild." Lila takes a sip from her cup. She wrinkles her nose. "No smiling e's, Cade."

I snort as Miers eyebrows dip in confusion.

"Not a beer drinker?" he guesses.

"Not really."

Miers turns, rummaging around on the counter behind him before presenting Lila with a bottle of tequila.

"We're going to be friends, Miers." She smirks, accepting the bottle and nodding toward a stack of cups. "Celebratory shot?"

"Damn, thirty-three, where you been keeping her?" Miers asks under his breath as Lila pours three shots.

I shake my head but can't help the grin that splits my face. I can already tell the guys on my team are going to adore her, probably fall a little in love with her, because she's so damn genuine.

"Congrats on your big, fat W." She raises her glass.

"Damn straight," Miers says, tapping his cup against hers. The three of us take the shot.

"Kristen! Sam!" she says suddenly, her eyes trained over my shoulder.

I turn to see a petite, cute brunette and a tall, lanky guy with bright green glasses enter the kitchen.

The girl, I assume Kristen, waves and pulls the guy, Sam, over to Lila's side. Miers and I step back, making room for

Lila's friends as she hugs them hello. "Thanks for coming," she whispers to the girl and I feel a swell of pride that she's here, with me, even though it can be overwhelming to have so many eyes watching your every move. But she's owning it.

"I never thought this would be my life," Sam mutters. "Or that I would meet you." He stares at me wide eyed. Pushing his glasses farther up on his nose, he holds out a hand. "I'm Sam."

"Cade." I shake his hand.

"Oh please. I know who you are. I mean, everyone knows who you are." He tilts his head, studying me. "You know, you're actually a lot hotter in person than you are in pictures. And that's really hard to do."

"Thank you," I reply, surprised by his directness.

He waves toward the brunette. "This is Kristen."

"Hi." She smiles shyly.

"Nice to meet you, Kristen. This is Miers." I smack a hand on Miers's shoulder, noticing how he checks out Kristen before he's pulled into another conversation. "Let me get you guys some beers." Walking over to the keg, I keep an eye on Lila. She relaxes completely, melting in between her friends, the three of their heads bent together, laughter erupting from their huddle.

10

LILA

C ade wasn't lying; this party is wild and rowdier then the college parties I'm used to. I've already witnessed three girls bend their heads together in a three-way kiss because a guy dared them to make-out, seen four penises, and have been offered cocaine. Twice.

Watching Cade work the room, slapping guys on the back, his signature chuckle rumbling, I'm impressed he manages to engage with this much attention. I'd be exhausted having so many people track my every move, hang onto my words, demonstrate an interest in me without really knowing me.

"He never lets you out of his sight," Kristen whispers in my ear.

Kristen, Sam, and I stand off to the side in the living room, essentially people watching, with small breaks for our own conversation.

"What do you mean?"

Her voice drops lower. "Even though he's talking with his friends and joking around, he keeps checking to make sure that you're having fun. He's totally aware of your presence."

Huh? Glancing up, Cade's gray eyes slam into me, simmering with heat that flares into a flame. His eyelids drop to half-mast, desire-fueled even from across the room. Drawing in a shaky breath, I blink and Cade's lips quirk with the tiniest movement, something between acknowledgement and need.

"Jesus." Sam shakes his head. "You guys really need a room. Like ten minutes ago."

His words do nothing to sever the intense, intoxicating pull between Cade and me. In fact, the longer we stare at each other with the adrenaline of Astor's win buzzing around us and the alcohol flowing freely, the more the invisible thread tightens, threatening to snap. Undeniable lust surges, and I bite my lip to stop whimpering from the look in Cade's eyes. Wiping my palms against my hips, I drag my eyes from his, inhaling to calm the inferno blazing to life inside.

"I'm going to vomit," Sam comments.

"Shut it," I scold him, but my voice shakes. Turning my attention back to my friends, I clear my throat. "What did you guys do after the game?"

"Got stuck in an absurd amount of foot traffic trying to get to King's for food," Sam offers.

"At least we ate," Kristen adds.

A loud, shrill voice erupts, interrupting our conversation and drawing our attention. I turn as a beautiful girl with bouncy, blond curls and a slamming body steps to Cade. Whining, she pushes her red-tipped fingernail deep into his chest, "How could you bring someone here?" Her eyes narrow into slits, scanning me from head to toe.

Cade rests his hand on the girl's forearm, inclining his head to the side of the room. The music cuts, amplifying the girl's shrieks so they carry throughout the first floor of the house.

"No!" she snarls, yanking her arm out of his grasp. "I don't understand how you could embarrass me like this, Cade."

"I think you're doing a pretty good job of that all by yourself," he chuckles.

Sam swallows his laugh, coughing.

A tear runs down the girl's cheek. "I thought we were together."

"Tamara," Cade sighs. "Can we speak privately?"

"No!" She smacks her palm against his chest. "Anything you have to say to me, you can say here, where everyone can see what a dick you are!"

"It's like that, huh?" Cade steps back until her hand slides off his chest.

"Yeah, it's like that." The girl spits, her embarrassment erupting into anger.

"Tamara, be real. We had dinner once. Last year. That was it. Besides, I thought you were seeing someone this summer?" he raises an eyebrow.

"I'm single now." She throws back as a few titters break out around the room.

"She's a snake," Kristen whispers.

"Savage," Sam agrees.

"So what, now you're off the market?" Tamara changes tactics, trying to corner Cade into a public declaration. "You just bounce from one blonde to the next, huh?" She jabs a finger in my direction, swinging the attention from her to me in an instant.

"Oh no," Kristen mutters.

Raising my cup to my lips, I gulp my beer, my toe tapping as I wait for Cade to shut this down. I'm not one to shy away from attention but I don't crave the spotlight either, not like this.

"Don't bring my girl into this."

Uh, what?

"Your girl?" Tamara repeats, her eyes boring holes into my skull.

"Yeah. This is my girl, Lila." Cade steps toward me and Kristen and Sam scoot out of the way. "She's with me so you all can stop with the whispers and the wondering. Gossip about something more important, like climate change."

Sam snorts.

But I don't turn to look. I can't move. Vicious stares and hushed conversations behind hands used as shields roll through the room.

What the hell just happened?

His girl?

With him?

My fingers dig into the red Solo cup I'm clutching.

What. The. Hell?

AFTER CADE'S PUBLIC DECLARATION, Kristen hustles me into a bathroom.

"Process that," she says, flipping the lock on the door.

"I'm going to hyperventilate." I sink to the closed toilet seat.

"Don't overanalyze this. I'm the only one who can do dramatic," Sam advises.

"He said his girl, right?" I ask for the fourth time. How could he say that out loud in front of all of those people? I mean, I've known him for like five seconds. Or a week. But still, this isn't middle school. No one declares a relationship status that quickly after the age of thirteen.

"I wonder if he'll update his Facebook status," Sam

muses. "That would really make it official. This…" he gestures to the party commotion outside the bathroom door "…is amateur hour."

I drop my head into my hands.

Sam leans forward against the sink, fiddling with his part in the mirror. "Do you think I should change my hairstyle?"

"Sam!" Kristen barks. "Focus. We're discussing Lila's life dilemma right now."

"What life dilemma?" Sam turns back around, hoisting himself onto the bathroom vanity. "This is amazing. Cade Wilkins just like, publicly claimed you. Enjoy it, babe. You know how many girls would love to be in your position right now?" He tilts his head. "Well maybe not sitting on a toilet during a party but—" A knock at the door interrupts him.

"Lila?" Of course it's Cade.

"What do I do?" I whisper to Kristen.

Her eyes widen and her mouth opens and closes a few times but no words come out. We stare at each other before the bubble bursts, and hilarity rains down on us. Erupting in laughter, I hunch over on the toilet, gripping my sides. Kristen's eyes are tearing as she tips over from her seated position guarding the bathroom door. "This is ridiculous." Kristen giggles.

"My friends are going to die," I agree.

Sam toes Kristen out of the way and swings the bathroom door open. "These two are your problem now."

Cade stands on the other side, his eyes dark and stormy, his jaw clenched, his lips smashed together in a flat line. Frustration rolls off of him, his muscles tensing and shifting as he braces himself against the doorframe. Linking his fingers on the top molding, he leans into the open space, his body a physical barrier, his stance a reminder that this isn't funny.

My giggles die as I drink him in. Kristen stands quickly, darting below Cade's arm, abandoning me with a behemoth glaring at me. Damn, I want to run my fingers up his abdomen, dig my nails into the ink circling his bicep, and drag my mouth along his unyielding jaw. I want to lose myself in his touch, his kiss.

But I don't do any of those things. I remain frozen on the toilet, my hands trembling until I sit on them.

Cade takes one stride into the bathroom and kicks the door closed behind him. The room shrinks, the air charging with a hum, the scent of lightening during a spring rainstorm perfuming the space. Crossing his arms against his chest, Cade's T-shirt pulls taut against his biceps. He rests his shoulder blades against the bathroom door, his ankles crossed. Even though his posture is casual, the energy he emits, the hurricane wreaking havoc in his eyes, is anything but breezy.

Sucking in a shaky breath, I cringe that I'm still huddled on the toilet. Springing to my feet, I square my shoulders, and meet his gaze head-on. Dark gray storm clouds swirl, uncontrollable. He bites down on the corner of his mouth, kicking one foot up behind him, the sole of his shoe banging against the door.

Standing my ground, I hold his tortured perusal, unwilling to blink first.

"Lila," he rasps, his eyelids hooded.

"Cade."

"Why'd you run?"

"I had to go to the bathroom."

The left side of his mouth twitches and he pushes off the bathroom door, another step closer to me. "No, you didn't. You couldn't get out of the room fast enough."

"You think?"

"It was shitty of me to put you on the spot like that in front of all those people."

"I told you I don't want a…thing." I gesture between us.

"I know. But this thing," he steps closer, crowding me, "it's not going anywhere."

I shuffle back until I'm pressed against the bathroom wall opposite the door. This damn bathroom is suffocating, overflowing with Cade's presence. Cade's forearm settles next to my head, boxing me in. His mouth is only inches from mine, his tongue darting out to swipe across his bottom lip.

I groan, my body involuntarily arching toward his. Jesus, what is wrong with me? And what is he thinking? Who could have a proper argument with all of these… distractions?

"I shouldn't have done that, blown up your spot, tossed all that attention your way. But fuck, babe," he drops his forehead to mine, his breath fluttering over my lips like an invitation I desperately want to RSVP yes to, "I hated that so many people threw shade your way. Every comment I heard pissed me off so much more because it was said about you, not me. And I won't let any of these people talk shit about you." He jabs a finger toward the party transpiring outside of the smallest bathroom that ever existed. "I'm not going to apologize for looking out for you."

"Cade," I'm breathless, quivering for him to stop talking and start touching. But I need to be strong, resolute … honest. "I'm leaving in four months. I don't do —"

"Serious, I know. Me either." His nose brushes against mine and I shiver. Shiver! "But give me a shot, Lila. I'm not going to wifey you. Just let me take you out, kick it with me, come to my games and rock my number, give it a chance."

"What if it's too much?"

His fingers close around my hips, tugging until my belly button is flush against his jeans. Jesus. His fingertips grip

The Last First Game

harder and need pools within me as his body grinds against mine. I whimper, desperate for relief from the wildfire consuming me.

"What if it's too damn good?" he angles his head lower, his bottom lip ghosting mine. "Let me light you up until we burn out. Babe, I'm not feeding you lines. I want you, Lovely."

My eyes flutter closed, my breathing ragged. I'm panting and still, Cade doesn't move. His thumbs draw circles into my hips, his mouth shadows mine, inhaling the desperation, the want, the need falling from my lips on each breath. I crave him, all of him, but he waits for me to say it.

"I want you, too. I do. But Cade, please."

"Please what, baby?"

"Don't ruin me."

His mouth descends on mine. I don't see it coming but I feel it, the particles in the space between us fragmenting, the air around us shrinking. His lips crash against mine and the back of my head hits the wall as I groan, this kiss like a drop of water against an inferno but still, a promise of more. The first move to tame the wild, uncontrollable fire within me.

Cade's hands drop from my hips to the backs of my thighs and he lifts me, stepping in between my thighs, pinning me to the wall. My arms snake around his neck, my forearms balancing on his shoulders. My fingers tug at the base of his neck and I grip my thighs tightly around his hips, grinding against him. He jerks forward, our teeth clashing, our tongues in battle with each other. He juts a knee underneath my ass to keep me from falling as one hand roams, dragging my shirt up and gripping my right breast. His squeeze dances the thin line of pleasure and pain, his touch stoking the fire raging through my bloodstream.

Slanting his mouth over mine, I suck on his tongue, bite his bottom lip and smile when he jerks back.

"You're dangerous, Lovely." His eyes smolder, and then he's on me again, his fingers exploring, his mouth tasting, his touch working me over until I'm teetering on the edge of the Grand freaking Canyon.

"Fuck." It falls from my lips like a plea and a curse and Cade drops his forehead to my shoulder, nipping at the sensitive skin along my collar bone.

"Jesus. I'm not going to fuck you for the first time against a bathroom wall at a house party," he mutters, clarity returning to the dimly lit room.

Slowly, I return to my body, my senses a jumbled mess of want and need and desperation. The fog lifts from my mind and I force my eyes open, taking in Cade's wild eyes, brimming with a hunger that borders on ferocious.

He lifts the cup of my bra over my breast and straightens my shirt. His fingers trace my skin, his eyes latched on mine. "You turn me inside out." The words are quiet, a confession. "I lose my head around you."

"Just, don't make me look stupid, okay? I like you, more than I should and more than I want to."

An unmistakable grin passes over his mouth but his eyes grow solemn. "Don't you get it, Lovely? You could straight up own me. When you break me, babe, just do it gently." He brushes a kiss against my forehead, reverent and surprisingly tender after the frenzy of clashing teeth and needy hands. "Tell me what you're thinking."

"Take me home, Cocky."

11

CADE

"Miss me?" I ask, as Lila catapults into my arms.

"Always," she dips her head to kiss me. "I can't believe you're leaving again tomorrow."

"Trust me, I'd rather be here with you than in South Bend, Indiana." I nip at her bottom lip, palming the backs of her thighs so I can lift her, deposit her on the corner of my desk, and settle in between her legs.

She swings her legs, playfully hooking her heels around the backs of my knees. I fall forward and she smirks. "Really? You'd rather listen to me talk about boring hospital rotations than kick Notre Dame's ass?"

"When you put it like that…" Bracing my arms on either side of her hips, I dip my head and capture her lips in a kiss that scorches as much as it soothes.

It's been two weeks since I called Lila out at that party, laying claim to a girl who doesn't want a label. Still, she's giving me a chance and I don't want to mess it up. For as much as I swore I didn't want a serious commitment, I'm seriously committing to her anyway.

Now when girls slide into my DMs with their nude photos

and not-so-subtle invitations, I hit delete. Passing up on the wild parties and laying off the alcohol, I'm over that scene. These days, the only woman I want naked in my bed is Lovely. The taste of her sweet skin and coconut perfumed hair is intoxicating enough.

Lila moans, her tongue swiping over my bottom lip. "Cade, don't make me beg for it."

I chuckle, lifting her easily. Spinning around, I toss her onto my bed, hovering over her. "I'd never make you do that." Lacing my fingers through her hair, I release her ponytail so her blond waves fan out across my pillow. Her blue eyes flare with arousal, brim with a thirst that I can quench.

Her fingers dance up my chest, pressing flat against my pecs before gliding down to my abdomen. She hooks her fingers under the hem of my shirt and teases it up.

"Hands up." She grins saucily, tugging my shirt over my head and tossing it onto the bedroom floor. "Damn, thirty-three." She flops back against the pillows, drinking me in like a desert wanderer wading into a lake. Her smile disappears as her eyelids grow heavy. Tracing the tribal tattoo that covers the left side of my ribcage, her fingers are cold against my skin and I hiss.

Two weeks of sleeping with Lovely, breathing in the scent of her shampoo on my pillowcase, sparring about important issues like the broken criminal justice system and universal healthcare, making her laugh so hard, soda shoots from her nostrils, has me craving more than just her body. I'm falling for her and it's like jumping from an airplane, unsure if the parachute will release.

Every moment is beautiful and vivid, filled with a rush of adrenaline, an appreciation for all the tiny details. But the faster I fall, the more anxiety fills my chest, weighing me down with panic. Will I float to a safe landing or crash and burn?

During moments like this one, with her laid out before me, dazzling eyes and full lips, I crave her more than my next breath and I need to cover her body with mine. To kiss her until she doesn't know her name, to lose myself in her so thoroughly that I won't know where she ends and I begin.

Dropping over her, my heartrate ticks up in anticipation, blood roaring in my ears. Her skin is smooth under my touch, her eyes shining like two sapphires. A vulnerability I want to explore flares in their depths before she blinks, tipping her chin up, and pulling me down by Jared's dog tags.

Jesus, I want this girl. With her, I want all the things I swore I never would… and the realization fuels me more than it frightens. Sweetness bursts in my mouth as I pepper kisses along her jawline, collarbone, the tops of her breasts. Undressing her, I peel off her sheer tank top as she shimmies her shorts down her legs.

Her hands are hot on my skin as she pushes down my shorts, removing my boxers with them. I take my time kissing every inch of her, my tongue tasting her skin, my lips molding to her curves. She squirms beneath me and I adore the tiny moans she breathes out.

Time shifts as the moments between us build and subside, flow and ebb. Fierce and languid, frenzied and leisure. This time when we connect, things are different. More.

Digging my fingers into her hips, a natural dance emerges between us, fusing our bodies, heightening everything about this experience. Strands of blond hair wrap around my knuckles, our mingled panting reverberates through me like a gong as I inhale coconut mixed with promise. Her lips are soft but hungry, my touch a confident caress. Our momentum propels us higher until we jump from the plane.

Parachute be damned.

She's all that matters.

And I'm lost inside her. Freefalling.

FLOATING ON A NATURAL HIGH, I cross into the end zone and secure our lead.

The wind whipping through my helmet, the rough leather of the football chafing my palms, the grass beneath my feet as I run down the field was once my greatest source of satisfaction. It's recently dimmed in comparison to falling asleep tangled up with my lovely, her hair tickling my chin, her snores puncturing the silence.

Tossing down the football as my teammates crowd me, yelling, cheering, and knocking against my helmet, I point at the scoreboard.

"Victory is ours!"

We beat Notre Dame 42-30.

Scouts reach out, showing up at my games. ESPN announces me as a projected NFL draft pick. Phone calls and congratulatory emails from friends back in Jersey pour in, overwhelming me with gratitude. My parents' pride and excitement humbles me, especially a photo Dad sends of Mama's expression when she sees me on ESPN.

I'm riding a natural high.

But at the forefront of my mind is wild blond hair and dazzling blue eyes.

Right now, I'm lost to reality.

And I don't care.

12

LILA

Football god, sex god, all I know is I am happy to kneel at the altar of Cade Wilkins.

"Lila?" Sam whistles, waving his hand in front of my face. "Where did you go?" he asks, pulling me back to the conversation at our lunch table.

"Hm?" I glance between him and Kristen.

"You're picturing him naked, aren't you? You are such a lucky bitch." He dips a French fry into his ketchup cup before popping it in his mouth. "I hate that I'm so jealous of you."

"Ahh, you're blushing." Kristen studies my face. "Y'all are cute."

"Don't be jelly. At least I shared the deets with you." I steal a handful of fries from Sam's plate.

"You gave nothing away. Nothing. Just 'I had sex with Cade.' I need more."

"I don't want you to hate me completely." I smirk at him, dunking a fry into his ketchup.

"I knew it. You really are a lucky bitch." He snickers, pushing his glasses up on his nose.

The ringing of my phone interrupts our conversation.

When Emma's face lights up my screen, I squeal. "Be right back," I tell my friends, answering the call. "Hey, girl, hey."

"Your boyfriend is on ESPN." Emma's excitement flows through the line.

"I know. He slayed against Notre Dame."

"Lila, I'm stalking him. He's hot. You're like, in a relationship, with a sex god."

I laugh, nodding until I remember she can't see me. "Em, he really is."

"Better than Steven?" she refers to my first serious boyfriend.

"Is that a joke?"

"Better than Jesse."

"Can we please stop calling him that?"

"What? It's not my fault you don't remember his name. He looked just like Uncle Jesse from *Full House*, pre-Aunt Becky."

"Okay, we don't need to do a rundown. Cade is … more. It's not just the physical with him, it's like, this emotional connection that's so…intense. We are totally in sync. I don't even know how to explain it; I've never experienced anything like it before. With anyone."

"Oh my God."

"I know."

"I'm so happy for you, Li."

"Thanks, love. What about you?"

"Le sigh. I need to meet someone."

"What about the tall guy from your Facebook photo?"

"Meh, I've got lots of little things happening but nothing really newsworthy to report."

"That's cryptic."

"I promise to divulge when I have something solid to share."

"Pinky promise?"

"Duh. When is Cade back?"

"Tomorrow."

"And …?"

"We have a date."

"Followed by hot sex?"

"Duh."

"You slay bae. The pact is in full effect." Muffled sounds drift through the line. "Sorry, girl. I've got to go. A little because I can't take any more of your gushing but mostly because the senator is due back from his meeting and I'm not supposed to be yacking on the phone."

"Tax payer dollars and all that?"

"Please, I'm not even getting paid. Message me this weekend?"

"Done. Love you."

"Love you. Talk soon!"

"'Bye, Em."

Before I can pocket my phone and rejoin my friends for lunch, it vibrates with a message.

Sex God: Pick you up at 7PM tomorrow Lovely?

Me: I'll be waiting. Miss you.

Sex God: Me too.

AT 6:53 PM, my stomach is rolling with nerves. I'm going to vomit.

"Stop being so jittery. You look hot." Kristen crosses her legs on her bed and leans forward. "Your outfit is fire. Just touch up your lip gloss."

"I'm nervous. Like, really nervous."

"Lila, he's already seen you naked."

"Gah! I know, that's the problem."

She raises her eyebrows, waiting for me to continue.

"I like him," I whine. "I mean, I really, really like him."

"This is a good thing." Kristen quirks an eyebrow. "Isn't it?"

"Yeah. I mean, it is. But I'm not supposed to like him. I'm living my best life, having an epic senior adventure. I'm leaving in December. I'm not supposed to want serious."

"You're changing your mind?"

"I'm changing my mind."

"So, tell him."

"I can't. I'm the one who said I didn't want a commitment."

"Lila." Kristen stands up and places her hands on my shoulders, shaking them a little. "You're allowed to change your mind. This is usually how relationships start, you know. Two people spend time together, learn more about each other, and if their feelings develop, then they want more from each other."

"I know, I know." I turn to give myself a once-over in the full-length mirror. I dressed up tonight, deciding on a short blue halter dress that flares from the hips and falls in delicate waves to the middle of my thighs. Slipping on nude sandals, I spin in front of the mirror and voice my real fear. "What if he shuts me down?"

"Stop being dumb."

"I'm not."

"You don't see the way he looks at you. By admitting your feelings, you're going to put him out of his misery."

"I'm going to vomit."

"Fine, let's say he doesn't want anything else. Then what?"

"My heart shatters into a gazillion little shards of disappointment."

I hear Kristen's eye roll, that's how loud it is. "You keep having a good time with a guy who makes you happy. But, Lila, that's not going to happen. Trust me, he wants more."

"We'll see." I muss the roots of my hair. I curled it tonight and it's fuller, cascading to the center of my back and around my shoulders.

"I would cut my left arm off for your hair," Kristen remarks, picking up a perfume bottle from her desk and turning to me. "Here." She sprays my neck and the inside of my wrists. "Now he won't be able to take his hands off you along with his eyes. You're welcome."

I snort, rubbing my wrists together and pressing them behind my ears to spread the scent.

A soft knock at the door causes us both to jump.

I scrunch my eyebrows at Kristen, but she shrugs her shoulders. "Sam?"

"He never knocks." I pull the door wide open and my heart freezes in my throat.

Cade. Standing at my dorm room door, a bouquet of flowers in his hand. He smiles and I melt. Right here, in a puddle on the floor. Dead.

"You win an award." Butterflies take flight in my stomach when I see the picnic he prepared for our date. That's right, a picnic. A full blown, after-dinner-we're-sipping-chilled-champagne-and-eating-chocolate-éclairs picnic.

"Nah, no award. I've never done anything like this before so I'm out of my element. Miers thought it was lame."

"Miers is single."

"There is that." Cade gestures for me to take a seat.

Sinking to my knees, I sit down on the colorful quilt.

Cade stretches out beside me, leaning back and glancing at the sky. "Trust me, I never thought I'd plan a picnic."

Uncapping a bottle of water, I take a sip, my throat dry.

"Hey, what's wrong?" Cade shifts his weight, turning his attention to me.

"Nothing. This is just, a lot. It's … impressive. I'm impressed." *Stop rambling.* Cade sits up, placing his hands on my bare thighs, his thumbs brushing back and forth. "Look at me."

Dragging my eyes up to his, I inhale sharply, flustered and flattered by the emotion ringing his irises.

"What's going on, Lovely?" he tugs on a strand of my hair, tucking it behind my ear.

"I think I love you." It comes out sharp and direct, like a bullet. *So unromantic.*

Cade averts his gaze, rolling his lips and pining them between his teeth.

"I'm sorry," I mutter.

He glances up, his head tilted to the side. "For thinking you love me?" A rumble moves through his chest and he looks away, until a snort of laughter escapes.

"You're laughing?" I accuse.

Shaking his head, Cade's laughter rings out, disturbing the quiet of the evening.

Embarrassment rocks through me. *Stupid, stupid, stupid.* Turning away, I drop my head, letting my hair rush forward like a shield.

"Lovely," Cade groans, his fingers finding my chin and redirecting my attention. "I know I'm in love with you. Me and you, it's for real, Lila. I'm not laughing at you. I'm laughing because I'm relieved you're finally catching on. Why are you squinting at me?"

"You're serious? You love me?"

"Lila Avers, I love you." Cade's voice is low. Husky. Confident.

"I love you too," I say, twisting my bangle bracelet around my wrist. "And it scares the hell out of me."

"Because it happened so quickly?"

"There's also that."

"Because you don't want anything serious?"

"Because I didn't want anything serious. Until you."

Cade reaches out and covers my trembling fingers with his hand, halting my jittery movements until I meet his gaze. His eyes are warm and sincere, melted silver. "Be my girl, Lovely. In every sense of the word."

"Like, your girlfriend?" I ask, clarifying because this would be an awful thing to misinterpret.

Cade nods, biting the inside of his cheek. "You're adorable. Why're you so nervous?"

"Because I want to be your girlfriend."

"Good. Let's do this for real."

"But what about…everything." I wave my hand, encompassing the entire park, LA, the state of California, the Virgo Supercluster. "You could be drafted to any team in the US. I'm supposed to apply to medical schools all over the country. I leave in three months to head back to Philly."

"Doesn't matter." Dipping his head, Cade leans forward until our foreheads touch. "None of it matters."

"Of course it matters. It's our futures."

"Okay, fine, it matters. But, none of the reasons you listed will stop the way I feel about you. Let's do this for real."

"Promise you won't ruin me?"

"Promise you'll be gentle?" he grins.

"I feel too much for you, Cade. Things between us are already so intense, so…real."

"I know what you mean. But Li, I swear, I'm not going to break your heart." He brushes the sweetest, most reverent kiss against my lips and I melt into him, my hands framing his face, the sting of his stubble scraping my palms.

"Be my girl, Lila," he whispers against my mouth and my eyes flutter closed. "For real. Not just a hook-up. Not just for this semester. Be my girl."

"Yes."

Cade's lips descend on mine and I capture his kiss; he tastes like hope and the final days of summer. Wrapping an arm around my back, he lays me on the quilt, hovering over my frame. Arching up, I trace his lips with my tongue until he grants me access to deepen our kiss. His fingers are lost in my hair, tugging, and my palms are dragging against the roughness of his jaw.

"Ever do it outside?" a whisper in my ear.

"Not much of an exhibitionist, Cocky."

"First time for everything." He bites down on my lip.

I tip my head back, and his mouth moves to my neck, my cleavage, his hands reaching up to untie my halter.

Pulling his T-shirt over his head, Cade's chest presses against mine, warming me from the chill in the night air. My hands track his body, ripple over the hard planes of his muscles, the smooth stretch of his back. Closing my eyes, I absorb every sensation: the gentle breeze, the scratch of the quilt against my back, Cade's accelerated breathing, the thunderous beating of my heart. His nose trails along my jawline before he pulls back, his eyes meeting mine, asking permission. The admiration flickering in his eyes makes me fall just a little bit faster. Harder. Deeper.

"You're perfect." The words are like a prayer in the quiet.

"Kiss me," I whisper and he shields my body once more.

He rocks into me slowly, languidly, like we have the entire night – our whole futures – before us. I arch into his touch, his fingertips pressing devotion into my skin, his mouth spilling tenderness into mine.

Time ceases to exist as I give myself up to this moment, to Cade, to my future with him. When we release, crashing down together, our palms are pressed as one, our hearts beating in sync, underneath a blanket of stars on a stretch of wildflowers.

13

CADE

Today, Lila is rocking my jersey for the first time. Number thirty-three flashing from her cheek and my name stretched between her shoulder blades, has me amped for game day.

Inhaling the fresh scent of grass, my mind runs through plays as we take the field, in high spirits for our home game against Stanford. Fans cheer wildly, the stadium packed with a pulsing wave of plum and gold.

Shielding my eyes from the sun, I scan the general vicinity of where Lila is sitting but it's impossible to pick her out among the thousands of fans. Knowing she's here for me is a heady realization and I vow to impress the hell out of her today.

At kickoff, my head is in the game. I reach for Jared's dog tags on impulse before remembering that I left them in my locker. Turning my attention to the play, I tune out the noise, my thoughts, everything that isn't football.

At the end of the first quarter, we're up 13-7 but it's too early to feel confident. With fifteen minutes until the half, we need to make some moves to gain more of a lead. Three minutes into the second quarter, Johnson throws a clean pass to me and I take off running. Blood pounds in my ears as I cross the thirty-yard line, my eyes trained on the end zone. Nearby, I hear the heavy breathing of a Stanford linebacker closing in and from my peripheral vision note one of our fullbacks advancing. Twinges of pain radiate throughout my right knee, shooting down into my shin as I will myself to move faster.

Stay hungry. Stay focused.

When a body slams into me from the back right, I don't see it coming. Clutching the ball into my abdomen as I roll forward, I protect the pigskin with everything I have.

A searing pain like fire and knives shoots through my knee, fragmenting throughout my leg, and I crumble, curling around the ball, the weight of other players landing on top of me, pressing my frame into the unforgiving Earth.

Inhaling dirt and grass, I freeze, unable to comprehend the excruciating pain that seizes me. My leg twitches, my knee throbs, the blood pounds louder in my ears. Bits of gravel dig into my skin, stinging my palms, which should be pushing me up now but lie pressed against the ground, useless. My breathing is muffled, warm air captured between the grass, my helmet, myself.

Far away, I hear a whistle, followed by a hush, a silence so penetrating I feel it in my bones.

I don't move.

"Wilkins?" Miers is on his knees next to my helmet. "Dude, can you hear me?"

Yes. I can hear you.

But the words don't come.

"Get the trainer. Now!"

In my peripheral vision, I see the fans on their feet. Their mouths in a shocked "O" like the Scream masks Jared and I wore for Halloween once. The silence grows louder.

It's deafening.

"Wilkins?"

"Cade?"

"Man, you okay?"

Nothing. I feel nothing but the suffocating weight of overwhelming pain.

And then, the plum and gold shimmer fades into weightless black.

My heartrate pounds in my chest, in my ears…in my knee.

My body falls slack.

Silence consumes.

A BLINDING light sears my eyes and I wince, the movement causing my body to jerk. My skin is on fire. *I'm burning!*

"Cade, take a deep breath and try to relax. You're at Henry Harper Medical Center. You were injured during the football game. We're doing everything we can to ease your pain," a voice says close to my ear.

The pain. Please stop the fire. My leg is in flames!

Lights flash in and out as black spots invade my line of vision.

Nothingness.

THE ROOM IS quiet when my eyelids flutter open. Shadows flicker across the wall, growing shorter with each blink. Closing my eyes, a beautiful blonde with dazzling blue eyes appears, her full lips curling up at the corners. She winks playfully, radiating sunshine.

My own breath surrounds me, shallow and coarse. A beeping breaks the silence of the room every few seconds.

The blonde reaches for me and I lift my arm to hold her hand except nothing happens. My arm doesn't move. Stepping toward her to close the distance, I glance down to find my feet firmly planted.

Nothing happens.

Nothing.

The room grows darker, quieter, emptier.

I'm out again.

14

LILA

D eafening.
   That's the silence of seventy-thousand people holding their breaths. No one speaks, no one moves. Not a fidget, barely a blink. We're all on edge, a bundle of connected nerves waiting, thinking, praying, and hoping. The silence is so intense, it sweeps the stadium like The Wave, but instead of bringing glee, it dispenses despair.

Number thirty-three is laid out.

Unmoving.

Number thirty-three is Cade.

He's facedown around the twenty-yard line, lifeless. His right leg is bent awkwardly at the knee. His teammates and coach huddle around him, the shouted questions and demands carrying throughout the silent field.

Time passes strangely. Stanford takes a knee. Cheer-leaders pause, their pom-poms clutched in front of their bodies.

Cade's helmet is worked off his head and his body is maneuvered onto a stretcher. He's carried off the field…and sound resumes. Abruptly and all at once. Like when you unplug headphones from a speaker.

The confused applause of fans.

It's not relief.

Cade hasn't moved.

He hasn't looked up.

He hasn't responded at all.

"Where are they taking him?" My hands clench and unclench, my entire being jittery. The paralysis I felt when Cade went down recedes and a desperation to move consumes me.

I need to see him.

"Henry Harper. Or the University hospital." Sam's hand feels warm in mine.

"I have to go."

"They'll never let you in. You aren't family."

"Then I'll wait."

It's irrational. I know it is. I've only been dating Cade for weeks. Hospitals never consider the girlfriends as family; they barely factor in fiancés and we are a long way from that.

But he couldn't wait to see me wearing his number after the game. Maybe he needs to see me just as much as I need to be with him.

"I'll go with you," Kristen offers, her arm wrapping around my waist. "Come on, let's get out of here before half-time. We'll wait together."

"Call me if you guys need anything." Sam squeezes my shoulder as I pass him on my way out of the aisle.

Kristen guides me down the bleachers, through pockets of people discussing Cade's injury in hushed tones. The game resumes but I don't look up; I can't bear to look at the foot-ball field if Cade isn't on it.

AFTER FOUR HOURS OF WAITING, I send Kristen home.

Sitting in a plain room lined with hospital chairs, my fingernails pierce half-moons in the armrests while my knee bounces up and down to an oppressive silence. A lukewarm cup of coffee from a vending machine sits on the table next to me, along with a magazine Kristen snagged from somewhere.

The team arrived immediately after the game. They were ushered into a private room, given updates by their coach, kept in the loop. No one noticed me.

I don't even know who won.

"Miss? Can I help you?" A nurse calls out from reception.

My neck snaps up and I glance around. *Is she talking to me?*

"Do you need help with something?

"I'm waiting for news about Cade Wilkins."

"That information is only available to family and his coach at this time. What's your name?"

"I'm Lila Avers—"

"Lila, there you are. I've been looking all over for you." Miers saunters over, pulling me out of my chair and slinging an arm around my shoulder. The weight of his arm is comforting and it centers me, reminding me that I have a right to be here. "We're down the hall." He turns toward the nurse, dazzling her with a smile. "Thanks for finding her for me."

"Oh, sure, no problem," the nurse stammers.

Miers starts for the hallway, pulling me along with him.

"How long have you been waiting?" He squeezes my shoulder, releasing me. His eyes scan my face when I don't respond. "Hey, you okay?"

"How is he? How bad is it?" My voice is both shrill and hoarse, uneven and shaky.

Miers's eyes soften and he sighs. "He's hanging in there. In a shit ton of pain but the doctors don't think the damage to his knee is structural. They're running a bunch of tests. He has a mild concussion and a stress fracture in his tibia."

The blood drains from my face. I'm pretty sure it pools in my feet because they're suddenly weighted, too heavy to lift and place down one step in front of the other.

Miers's eyebrows dip. Bending at the knees, he lowers himself until we're eye level. "He's going to be fine. Really."

Releasing the breath I didn't realize I was holding, my body sways as relief surges and I stumble.

Miers steadies me. "You're really worried about him, aren't you?"

"Can I see him?"

"Yeah, I think you're probably the only person who could cheer his moody ass up. Come on."

Following Miers down the hall, I collide into his back when he stops short outside one of the hospital rooms. Inclining his head toward the door, he says, "I'll be on the lookout for any mean nurses. Try and cheer him up."

Holding my breath in my lungs, preparing for the worst, I push into the hospital room. "You're awake." I stumble on air.

"Lila." Cade's eyes widen, his hands gripping the rails of the hospital bed as he sits forward, wincing in pain.

"Hey. Don't move."

"Get in here, Lovely." He grasps the arm rest of a chair next to his bed and drags it closer to his bedside. "How did you get past the nurse? Miers told me she's menacing."

Exhaling the biggest sigh in the history of the universe, I

beeline to his side. Grabbing his face, I kiss his forehead, his cheeks, even his eyelids, before pressing my lips against his.

Sitting on the chair, I point to the number thirty-three on my jersey. "What? You thought I'd let you miss out on seeing me rock this jersey just because you passed out?"

Cade laughs, the sound lighting me up from the inside until I'm pretty sure I'm glowing like a neon sign that says 'I'm in love with this guy.'

"God, babe, I'm happy you're here. Thank you." He grasps my hand, bringing it to his lips and kissing my knuckles. "And you look sexy as hell rocking the thirty-three." Shifting in the bed, he tugs me closer, grimacing, "I'm pretty hopped up on pain meds right now so I can't be held accountable for my actions."

"Is that right?"

Dragging my face down to his, he kisses me hard. Underneath the pressure of his mouth, I taste the sourness of desperation, of fear.

15

CADE

Two days have passed since my injury on the field. Two long ass days. The stress fracture in my tibia is a joke compared to what's really going on. I've heard whispers and musings and while nothing has been confirmed, I know in my soul that the whispers contain a chilling truth.

I should have been casted and discharged by now. Instead, my leg is splinted while doctors continue running a multitude of tests. Something darker is at play. It's the type of darkness no one says aloud without confirmation but I suspect what the doctors think.

Cancer.

Mama called last night, sobs wracking through the phone line. Of course, she wanted to fly out to take care of me. I lied to my mama; I told her my injury is under control and I'd be back on the field in no time. Finally, I understand the silence and the whispers, because there's no way I'm going to shatter my mama's heart without confirmation.

So, I embrace the denial with outstretched arms, knowing my life is about to come crashing down and when it does, it's going to pull me under with it. Focusing on my little ray of

OCTOBER

sunshine, I cling to Lila, also knowing that my time with her is running out.

———

ON THE THIRD DAY, I'm desperate. I crave the dirt, the grimy grit of the football field, the feel of a pigskin in my hands, the sound of the wind rushing past as I run toward the end zone.

When Dr. Somers enters my room after lunch, I sit up straighter in my bed. Studying his grave expression, my suspicions are confirmed before he opens his mouth. Inhaling, ice cubes pack together in my chest like a giant snowball. My throat is too dry to swallow. Clenching the rails of my hospital bed, I brace myself for the blow.

"Cade."

"Dr. Somers."

He places his hands on the bar at the foot of my bed. "We need to talk."

"Tell me straight. No sugarcoating." Anxiety pulses in my eardrums, growing louder with each passing moment of not knowing.

But knowing.

"We have to do a biopsy for confirmation, but we found a tumor in your proximal tibia. The tests are indicating Osteosarcoma."

"Cancer."

"Cancer."

"In my leg?"

"In your tibia. That's this bone here. The one you fractured in the game." Dr. Somers's hand indicates the lower portion of my leg. "It's responsible for supporting your weight and knee joint, which is why you've been experiencing so much soreness in your knee."

"How bad?" What does that even mean? My fingers tremble against the stark bed sheets. I curl my hands into fists.

"We'll have to biopsy the tumor to gain a better under-standing of what we're dealing with. At this time the prognosis seems positive, and I think you will make a full recovery. The cancer hasn't spread to any other organs or to your lymph nodes. However, the cells are abnormal and can spread quickly, meaning we have to act fast."

"What are you suggesting?" I clear my throat, plucking the skin next to my eye.

"First, we will perform a needle biopsy to grade the tumor. Depending on the results, we'll develop a strategy. At this time, we will most likely start with several cycles of chemotherapy to shrink the size of the tumor. Right now, it's measuring at ten centimeters. Shrinking it will make resecting it easier. After the chemo, we will perform surgery to remove the tumor in its entirety. Following surgery, you will undergo additional cycles of chemo-therapy."

"Why the chemo afterwards, if you think you can get it all?"

"To make sure that there are no bits of cancer that aren't showing up on the imaging tests. Sometimes it happens." He sighs. "Also, the chemotherapy will help reduce the chances of the cancer recurring after surgery."

"Will you have to take my lower leg?" Panic rises in my chest. Never mind playing football again, I'll be lucky to walk.

"Not at this stage. But, we need to act immediately since the tumor is already measuring at ten centimeters and is likely to grow quickly."

"So I'll walk again?" A twinge of hope blossoms in my

stomach and I push it down, fearful if I let it bloom that I'll be crushed later, when I can't even stand up.

"I think you'll make a full recovery." He pauses. "In terms of normal, everyday activities like walking, going up and down stairs, eventually, even working out. But you will have to work up to this. Rehabilitation is a long road and even with limb-salvage surgery, it will take close to a year to learn how to walk again. To play football again, this will be more difficult to achieve."

"But not impossible."

"Not impossible, no. But not likely either."

Breathing out, I lean my head back against the pillow and close my eyes. The ice cubes in my chest expand, threatening to choke me. *I may never play football again.*

"Let's not get ahead of ourselves." Dr. Somers reins me back in. "One step at a time. This is a long process, Cade." His eyes hold mine in warning.

"When do we start?"

"As soon as possible. I scheduled your biopsy for tomorrow."

Whistling under my breath, numbness spreads through me, freezing my emotions and leaving me with … logic.

Dr. Somers pats the railing of my bed. "I know I've given you a lot to think about and consider. Take some time. But before I go, do you have any questions?"

"No. Thank you, Dr. Somers."

"I'll be back tomorrow morning to check on you."

"Okay."

At the door, he turns. "Make sure you talk to someone about this. Anyone. A professional here at the hospital, your family, friends, teammates, coach, girlfriend, whoever. But don't keep it bottled up. You're going to need a strong support system going forward."

"I will."

After he leaves, I clench the sheets as tightly as I can, my hands straining painfully. The pain, the physical exertion feels good. Hanging my head, the ice cubes melt, flood my chest with questions I don't know how to answer.

16

LILA

"You're shutting me out." My tone is accusatory as I perch on the edge of Cade's bed, willing him to meet my eyes.

"I'm not shutting you out." He keeps his tone light but it's bullshit because he doesn't look at me. "I don't have anything to tell you."

"Cade."

"Lila." He looks up, his eyes hard and flinty and nothing like melted silver. "I've been in this hospital for a week. I'm going stir-crazy. I know I'm in a shitty mood and I don't want to take that out on you, on anyone, so please, don't interrogate me."

"I'm not interrogating you." Crossing my arms over my chest, I shrink into myself. "I'm worried about you. Am I not allowed to be concerned that my boyfriend has been laid up in a hospital bed for a week and isn't really talking to me?"

"Of course, babe. I'm sorry." He pulls me into a hug and pats my back but it feels wrong.

He's placating me.

"Distract me, baby." Cade strokes my hair as I pull out of our embrace. "Tell me something good."

"Cade, talk to me."

"I am. Tell me about your day. How's your internship? You're in pediatrics now, right?"

Swallowing back the tears that claw at my throat, I nod.

"Do you like working with kids?" he asks, ignoring the tension between us.

Each day, the chasm between us widens. Soon, it will be so large, I won't be able to reach his side without falling into the divide. I hate the uncertainty that colors our conversations, the unknown that hangs over our interactions. Something dark is coming.

Does Cade feel it too?

"THANK GOD IT'S FRIDAY! What are you up to tonight?" Kristen opens the locker next to mine in the staff locker room and drops her lanyard inside. "Interning sucks."

"Tell me about it." I shelve my notes.

"You're not going to study this weekend?"

"I need a time out from my life."

Kristen plops onto a bench. "Any word from Cade?"

"Just the usual. He keeps acting like everything is fine when it obviously isn't. And instead of confiding in me, he's pulling away but under this pretense of pleasantries. It's infuriating." I sit down next to her, kicking at the ground.

"Bad day?"

"Bad week. My dad moved his girlfriend in with him. My mom is losing it. And I don't care about any of this." I gesture to the locker room, but really mean the hospital and my internship in it. "I just want to go home, pull on sweats, crawl into bed, and sleep for a million years."

"I have a better idea."

"I doubt that."

"Come on, Lila, what you need is a night out." Kristen clutches my forearm, turning me toward her.

"The last thing I need is to be surrounded by happy, annoying people, living their best lives."

"I'll buy all your drinks."

"Jesus, I must really seem desperate."

"More depressed but desperate works too."

Rolling my eyes, I consider her suggestion.

"It will be fun. A girl's night plus Sam." Kristen continues, shaking my arm as if that's going to make me say yes.

It does. "Fine."

Kristen squeals, dropping my arm and clapping her hands together. "Trust me, it's going to be fun. You need this."

HOURS LATER, Kristen, Sam, and I occupy bar stools at a dive bar near campus. The live band starts their next set and the noise of the bar ticks up. Even though smoking is forbidden inside, the space has a hazy feel to it, as if everyone is here for the same reason: to make bad decisions.

"Ugh," Sam groans into his mojito. "I hate seeing Cliff every day. It's a cruel world that I have to see his delectable body and know exactly what I'm missing."

"My ex-boyfriend has a new girlfriend. She's blonde." Kristen squints an eye at me. "Kind of looks like you."

Sam snorts.

"You guys aren't cheering me up at all."

"Didn't realize that was the point of our night out." Sam points a finger at me and I grab it, twisting his hand.

"Fair enough," I concede. "But I can't do any more depressing chat today. For the first time in weeks, we're out, among the living, and not in dingy hospital halls following orders. Let's stop bitching about guys we're over." I fix them both with a pointed stare. "And have some actual fun. Kristen was right, I need this." Waving over the bartender, I toss a fifty on the bar. "Three shots of Patron please."

Sam twirls his straw around in his mojito. He pushes his glasses up on his nose and squares his shoulders. "I hate when you're right, Li. But, you are."

"I know."

We look at Kristen. "Oh all right. I know this was my idea and now I'm being the Debbie Downer. Let's drink."

When the shots arrive, we sprinkle salt on our wrists and each take a wedge of lime. "To tonight." Kristen raises her shot glass.

"To having fun," I add.

"To new, sexy men," Sam announces.

Snorting, I toss back the shot, welcoming the burn of the alcohol, desperate to feel something good.

After a few more rounds, we barhop. The next bar on our list, Stella's, is packed. A makeshift dance floor pulses with bodies in front of a low stage where a local band plays popular covers. The floor is slippery from spilled drinks, and I almost fall as Kristen slides in her wedges and grabs my arm.

"Sorry, Li."

Waving away her apology, I hold her up, thankful I didn't wear heels.

Sam walks up behind us, balancing a triangle of tall

glasses between his hands. "Sex on the Beach." He passes one to me and I release Kristen.

"I haven't had one of these since, like, high school."

"This is a proper night out, baby doll. It's the only time you can respectably drink these, so you may as well enjoy it."

Clinking glasses with Sam, I take a sip. The sugary sweetness coats my throat, bringing me back to the summer before college. The summer before I met Maura, Mia, and Emma and finally discovered true friendship.

Kristen shrieks again, sliding on the slick floor as she dances. The band takes a break and salsa music floods the speakers.

Sam hands off the other two glasses to me and grabs Kristen. "Time for dancing, sweetheart." Twirling Kristen, he whisks her into the midst of the crowded dance floor.

Moving to one of the high-top tables, I place down our drinks and reach into my purse for my cell phone.

"Hey," a familiar voice says as an arm slings around my shoulders.

I look up into Miers's clear eyes.

"Hey yourself." I gesture to the glasses on the table. "Thirsty?" I offer him Kristen's glass, knowing she doesn't need the extra liquid courage.

He removes his arm from my shoulder and picks up the glass. When he takes a sip, his face contorts in disgust. "What is that?"

"Sex on the Beach."

"Oh wow. And here I thought you were classy. Are you serious with this?" He shakes the glass in my face.

"Standard fare for a girl's night out."

"Oh, is that what this is?" He looks around, amused. "Where are your girls?"

"Dancing."

"And you're standing here by yourself?"

"Now, I'm talking to you."

Miers chuckles, pulling his hand down over the back of his neck. "And I guess I'll have to entertain you until your friends reappear?" he asks, shooting daggers at a guy who bumps my arm as he passes by.

"That'd be the gentlemanly thing to do."

He takes another sip of the drink.

"Growing on you?" I guess.

He nods, his eyes crinkling in the corners. "Yeah, but don't tell anyone."

"Yo, there you are." A hulk with bulging biceps and dreadlocks hands Miers a beer.

"Thank the Lord." Miers winks at me, trading the Sex on the Beach for a Corona.

I cough, rolling my eyes at him.

"Hendrix." Miers turns toward the tower of steel. "This is Lila. Lila, Hendrix."

"Lila? Cade's girl?"

"That's me."

"Hey. Good to finally meet you." He offers me his large hand and while I expect his grip to crush my fingers, his squeeze is surprisingly gentle.

"So," Miers tilts his head toward me, "talk to Cade today?"

"Just a few text messages." I lift my chin toward the dance floor. "I got roped into a night out with my friends."

Hendrix follows my line of sight, zeroing in on Kristen. "You've got a beautiful friend."

"Simmer down," Miers cuts him off. "You gonna call Cade?"

What is this? Twenty Questions. The serious tone of

Miers's question raises my suspicion. "Why? Is something wrong? Did something happen?"

Miers averts his gaze immediately. "Nah. I mean, you know. Just make sure you give him a call. I'm sure he'd like to hear from you."

Hendrix also avoids eye contact, pretending to be fascinated by the horrid upholstery of the nearby chairs.

I grab Miers's hand, tugging until he looks at me. "Is he okay?"

"Yeah." He fakes a smile. "Just give him a call tomorrow, okay?"

"Of course."

"Lila!" Kristen's petite frame hurdles into me, and I bump into the table, knocking over the three glasses. "I'm drunk as a skunk!" She wraps her arms around me. "I'm so happy you're my friend."

Miers and Hendrix chuckle. Sam stands off to the side, his eyes ogling Hendrix. Oh jeez.

"Well, guys, it was good to see you. We better grab a cab and get this girl home." I nod to the hysterically laughing bundle of Kristen in my arms.

"Yeah. Good luck with that." Hendrix smirks.

"See you around, Lila." Miers throws over his shoulder as he and Hendrix move into the crowd, their heads towering above everyone else.

Sam pinches my side. "Next time, introduce me!"

"Next time, scrape your jaw off the floor."

"Fair point. Okay, I think it's time for Kristen to sleep this off."

"You think?"

We box Kristen in between us as we make our way out into the breezy air of October and hail a cab.

"How'd you know I love munchkins?" I ask Lila as she slips into my hospital room, balancing a box of Dunkin' Donuts munchkins and a tray with two coffees.

She peeks around the door into the hallway and then closes it quietly before turning to face me.

"You look like you're about to commit a crime."

"I'm technically not supposed to be here." She holds up her hospital ID.

"You're secret's safe with me."

She rolls her eyes, and the tightness pinching them subsides. "I'm glad you're awake. I was worried it's too early."

"Nah, I can't sleep. I haven't spent this much time alone since I had mono when I was sixteen."

"Kissing too many girls?"

"You know, it was just one girl. Daniella Martino. She gave me freaking mono." I'll never forget the look of horror that passed over Mama's face when she learned I had the kissing disease. Or Dad and Jared's hysterical laughter.

"From just one kiss!" Lila's face contorts in mock horror.

"All chocolate?" I gesture toward the munchkins.

"An assortment." She places the munchkins on my bedside table and lays a napkin out on my stomach. Then she hands me a coffee. As an afterthought she asks, "You don't have any dietary restrictions or anything, do you?"

"Now you ask?" I reach into the box for a chocolate munchkin, popping it into my mouth.

"Do you?" she presses, her eyes wide.

"No, relax." I pat her knee as she sits on the chair next to my bed. "Thank you for bringing breakfast. It's a welcome change from the hospital food." Sipping the coffee, I roll the bold roast around in my mouth before swallowing. "I miss real coffee. Hospitals should really step up their game on the coffee front."

Lila helps herself to a munchkin, biting into it thoughtfully, leaving a trail of powdered sugar around her lips and on her chin. I grin at her, wiping at my own face. She cracks a smile, taking my hint and dragging the back of her hand across her mouth. "Sorry," she mumbles.

"So, how've you been? What'd you do last night?"

"I went out with Kristen and Sam."

"How was that?"

"Kristen got smashed. Poor girl is hurting today. Sam made us drink lots of sweet, sugary, girly drinks."

"He should know my girl only drinks tequila."

"Exactly," Lila says off-handedly, worry lines bracketing her mouth.

"What's up?" I press the button on the side of the hospital bed to lift the headrest until I'm sitting up straight.

Lacing my fingers with hers, she says, "I saw Miers and Hendrix at Stella's last night."

"Did they hit on you?" I tease.

"No, nothing like that."

I squeeze her fingers. "Ask me."

Big, blue, soulful eyes I could drown in shimmer and dazzle with unshed tears. She's beautiful, even when she's hurting. "Are you okay?" We both know that saying the words aloud will make them real. True.

"No." My voice is steady, the clarity of it ringing in my eardrums.

Lila's tears tip over, gliding down her cheeks in silent protest. Raising my fingers to her face, I stop them in their tracks. "Lovely, I need you to ask me."

"How bad?"

My chest squeezes at the break in her voice. I take a fortifying breath. *This is it.* "It's cancer." I watch her breath shudder in her chest, her shoulders rolling forward as if to protect herself from an external threat. But it's me; I'm the threat. I'm hurting her after I swore I wouldn't. "Osteosarcoma. I got my biopsy results yesterday."

Lila hangs her head, her hair falling forward to hide her eyes. Her breath catches and she whispers words I can't make out, although her tone overflows with anguish. Her hand falls limp in mine.

"Baby." I shake her fingers until she looks up. "Come here." I flip back the blanket covering my legs and gesture to the space next to me.

"I … I can't."

"Of course you can. I promise you'll feel better." I pull her hand until she shifts to the edge of my bed. "Lila?"

She shakes her head quickly before dropping her head onto my chest and curling into my side. The napkin flutters to the floor as her arm fastens around my waist, holding on tightly, holding me together. Gathering her in my arms, I hug her to my chest, gliding my hand up and down her back as she cries.

Sobs of anguish. They wrack her body and reverberate through mine. An ache that crushes in its intensity spreads through me, followed by a sweeping coldness. What the hell am I doing? I can't put my lovely through this.

She told me she didn't want to do serious her senior year of college.

It doesn't get much more serious than this.

And I'd be a selfish dick to allow her to suffer along with me just because she'd feel too damn guilty giving up on us.

I hug her tighter, allowing myself these moments to feel her warm skin, to breathe in the coconut of her hair. My stomach roils, empty and hollow, as I reconcile what I have to do with what I want to do. Our time together was too damn short and yet it made me crave more, had me yearning to share my day and plan a future with her.

Right now, none of that is possible.

Dread bundles in my veins and I feel sick, shivering. Lila raises her tear-stained face, the tip of her nose red like cherry ice. "Are you cold?"

"I'm fine."

"Cade, I'm sorry." She drags the back of her hand across her mouth. "I'm so sorry you're sick. And I'm, I'm lying here hysterical while you're, you're—"

"Shh, it's okay. I wanted to tell you myself." My thumbs swipe the moisture underneath her eyes, and I bite down on the inside of my cheek to keep the emotions clawing at me from surging forward. "You're mesmerizing. So beautiful, even when you cry."

A small smile flickers over her lips and there she is, my sunshine peeking out from behind a storm cloud.

"I'm going to be fine, Lovely."

"Really?"

"Really. My doctor is confident that he can remove the

entire tumor. It's not going to be easy, but it's not impossible either," I repeat Dr. Somers words.

"I'll be here. You know that, right?" Her eyes dart over my face, her hands gripping my T-shirt. "I know we haven't been together for that long, but I love you, Cade. I'm not going anywhere."

My throat constricts. The damn ice cubes are back, blocking out my ability to breathe. How do I tell her we won't last? We're not supposed to. Not when she needs to embrace her final year of college, apply to medical schools, and seize all the exciting things ahead of her.

A lump forms in my throat, making speech impossible. Instead, I drink her in, commit the lines and angles of her face to memory.

She leans forward and kisses me with a reverence I don't deserve.

And it damn near breaks me.

Groaning into her mouth at the unfairness of it all, I thread my fingers through her hair and fuse my lips with hers. Pouring everything I feel, all that I am, into this kiss, time stops. For one blink, we're not in a hospital bed. I'm not sick, and she's not crying.

I'm just a guy desperately in love with a woman I can't have.

18

LILA

"Cade has cancer."

"What?" Emma's voice drops to a whisper. "What do you mean? Wait, where are you?"

"I'm in the hospital bathroom. He's sick." Glancing at my reflection in the mirror, splotchy skin, puffy eyelids, and a red nose greet me.

"What's his prognosis?"

"It's Osteosarcoma. He has a tumor in his leg. I don't know, the doctors are confident they can remove it but he will still have to undergo chemo and, Emma, what the hell?"

"I don't know, babe. That's insane and awful and I am so sorry. Thank God they caught it now, while it's still operable."

Swallowing a lump of tears, I screw my eyes shut. "That's true. I know."

"How's he doing? Li, you're going to have to be there for him."

"He's cracking jokes! All smiles, comforting me while I climb into his bed and sob like an emotional train wreck. I wasn't strong, Em. I wasn't supportive or helpful or anything. I was a mess. I *am* a mess."

"Lila, it's okay. Stop. You're entitled to your feelings and reactions; you do have a heart."

"I know. But I – I cried. He told me and I cried." I palm my face, my fingers slipping off from the amount of moisture.

"Of course you cried. You're allowed to have feelings, Lila. Just, take a minute. Take some deep breaths and relax. And be there for him when he needs you."

"Right," I say unconvincingly.

Dragging a mouthful of air into my lungs, I wipe my face with a paper towel. With Emma's chatter in the background, I begin to calm down.

"You're going to be okay, babe. Be there for your guy and we'll be here for you."

"Thanks, Em. I have to go." I look down at my phone, rolling my eyes when a text from Dad comes through.

Dad: Lila, please get in touch. I'm leaving for Newport next weekend. We need to talk before I go. It's important.

Ugh, he seriously has the worst timing.

What could be more important than Cade?

"Okay. Call me if you need anything, Lila."

"Yeah, thanks." I hang up and finish drying my eyes. Then, I hurry to meet Sam for rounds.

LEAVING THE HOSPITAL AFTER LUNCH, I step into the sunshine, inhale the fresh air, hold it in my lungs, and expel the heaviness that's been choking me since my conversation with Cade.

How long has it been since Cade breathed in clean air and sunshine?

I catch the bus back to my dorm, sliding into a window seat so I can watch the trees pass outside.

Sex God: Lila, thanks for coming this morning. I'm glad we talked in person. I know it's a lot to process. Let me know if you want to talk about anything. If I don't answer, it's because I'm sleeping off the sugar coma from too many munchkins. ;)

Resting my head back, I squeeze my eyes shut, frustrated with his flippancy, touched by his sweetness. I don't want him to worry about me. I want to worry about him, comfort him, show up for him.

Should I make a care package? What would I put in it? What's his favorite movie? Or book? Now that shit got real, it dawns on me how little I know about Cade. Sure, our physical connection is fire. Yes, he understands me and makes me feel whole. But just because I love him doesn't mean I know how to best support him.

He needs to focus on his well-being, his recovery, himself. I can't be a pathetic mess distracting him with my emotional outbursts. I need to show up, be strong, be…more.

When I arrive back at my dorm, I strip down to my underwear and snuggle into one of Cade's oversized hoodies. Breathing in his scent, I weave it into my subconscious and collapse into sleep, giving my overactive mind a much-needed reprieve.

19

CADE

"Yo. Good, you're awake." Miers walks into my hospital room.

"What's up, man?"

"Oh, I love Dunkin'." He peers into the box of munchkins on my bedside table and snags three chocolate doughnut holes before dropping into the chair next to my bed.

"Bastard. You know they're my favorite."

"Where'd you get them from anyway? Hitting on the nurses already?"

"Nah, man. Lila dropped by this morning."

His head snaps up. "Did she?"

"I know you saw her last night, bro. What happened?"

He sighs, lifting his baseball hat off his head, running his hand over his hair, before dropping the hat back down the way he always does when he's stressed. "Hendrix and I ran into her at Stella's. She was standing by herself since her friends were dancing, so I thought I'd chat with her for a bit. You should have seen the guys circling her. If I walked away, she'd get eaten up like chum during shark week."

My face stiffens, my hands curling into fists as anger

blazes through my bloodstream, hot like lava. Of course guys hit on Lila, how could they not? But it's me not being able to shield her from the unwanted attention, from not being able to do jack shit, that pisses me off.

"Sorry."

"For telling the fucking truth?" I snap, looking out the window.

"Anyway," Miers wisely moves on, "I asked her if she'd talked to you and she immediately knew something was up. Sorry, dude. She's perceptive as hell, even drunk."

"How drunk was she?"

"Not nearly as drunk as her friend. That girl was sloshed." Miers shakes his head, chuckling. "Really cute though."

"How did she get home?" Protectiveness surges, replacing my anger. I hate that there's no way I can get to her if she needs me.

"Cab. She was with friends. I'd never let her leave alone, you know that."

"Yeah."

"So what happened when she showed up this morning?"

"I told her." My voice falls flat.

"And?" He sounds exasperated.

I drag a hand over my jaw, scratching the stubble around my mouth. "She cried."

"She really cares about you, dude. I know it hasn't been that long for you guys but Lila, she's legit."

"Yeah, she is," I admit, looking away to control all the emotions that keep swarming me. Anger, frustration, sadness, anxiety, fear…it's exhausting. Downright draining.

"What's up, dude?" Miers asks, leaning forward and resting his elbows on his knees.

"I gotta cut her loose." The words are monotone when

they come out of my mouth, which is for the best since I need to keep my feelings out of this decision.

"What the hell are you talking about?"

"Lila."

"Cut her loose? Are you for real? That girl is in love with you and –"

"Exactly. She's in love with me. I may not be here in a few months." My tone is venom and Miers jerks back.

"Don't say that shit, thirty-three. You've got a favorable prognosis and –"

"Favorable? Is that what we're calling it? Miers, the next year of my life is going to be one big fucking question mark. It's going to be long and unpredictable with a million ups followed by a billion downs. Would you bring a girl you love, the one you could see your whole damn future with, along for that? A beautiful, intelligent, passionate woman with big plans and even bigger dreams? Would you cuff her to the same goddamn hospital bed you're shackled in?"

Miers glares at me, unblinking, but he doesn't refute my questions.

"Would you?" I press.

"Fuck dude, I don't know what I'd do, alright? But I don't think shutting Lila out is going to help you or her. Or your healing. You need her, man."

"Yeah, I need her to be happy. To be whole."

"She's happy with you."

"Maybe right now, right this second. But what about in a few months when she's back in Philadelphia with her friends? What about when they're planning a senior trip and she can't go because her boyfriend is dying in a hospital bed and she feels guilty? What then?"

Miers pinches the space between his eyebrows and pops a munchkin into his mouth.

"What then?" I repeat.

"I don't know! I'm stress eating now." He looks around my hospital room, "Let's get out of here."

"What?" My face snaps up to his. "I can't just leave, Miers."

A knock sounds on my door and Miers and I both look as Dr. Somers enters my room.

"Dr. Somers, is everything okay?" I lean forward, catching the smirk Miers tosses my way.

"I'm springing you from here, Cade."

"What?"

Miers snickers. "Want to grab a beer and wings?"

"Only one beer." Dr. Somers holds up one finger. "You can go home, take some time with your family and friends. You start chemo next week."

"Is this a joke?" My eyes swing between Dr. Somers and Miers. "You knew?"

Miers shrugs as Dr. Somers explains, "Who else was going to take you for that beer? Michelle will be in shortly to take out your IV. I'll see you soon, Cade. Maybe grab a Heineken. Something about smiling e's." He shakes his head, chuckling, as he leaves my hospital room.

"Dude, let's pause the serious, life-changing decisions and get out of here. We're heading to Anchor's Tavern. Steaks, burgers, beers, fries. Hendrix is meeting us there even though he'll complain the entire time about his buffalo sauce being better."

Emotion swells in my throat. "That sounds...fucking perfect, man. Thank you."

"No worries, dude."

20

LILA

Brandon: *Dad and Brenda moved in together. Just a heads up. Mom's having a tough time with the news.*

Emma: Hey, how's your guy? Chat this weekend?

Dad: Lila, call me. Brenda and I are leaving for Newport. I have something to tell you.

Miers: Hey, Cade is home and settled in. He's giving his parents a call to discuss his treatment so give him a minute before you come by.

Kristen: Break out the wine! I have a date!

Me (to Kristen): Come home right now! Wine is waiting.

Relief.

It rocks my system, shocking me to my core, but there it is. Shouldn't I feel something else – a lot of somethings when my family is falling apart, Miers is texting me instead of Cade, and I have no plans for tonight? Shouldn't I be concerned, angry, and depressed?

Instead, I'm wildly relieved to sit in my tiny dorm room and drink wine. Reaching into my bedside table, I pull out a corkscrew and a stack of cups before retrieving a bottle of wine from my closet.

"I have huge news," Sam announces, waltzing into my dorm room as I uncork the wine bottle.

"Please tell me it's good news."

"The best. Like, ever."

"Spill it." I pour him a glass of wine and hand it to him before taking a large gulp of mine. Sitting cross-legged on my bed, I hunch forward in anticipation. Sam sits across from me, leaning back against my pillows.

"I have a date!"

"With who?"

"The hot law student who wears Hugo Boss socks and can coherently speak about the minimalism of Miuccia Prada's new line." He drapes his hand over his brows. "I think I'm in love."

"Chris Martello?" I guess, picturing the only law student I know who fits Sam's description. Chris is tall, has a twelve-pack, dresses in all designer, and always has an Earl Gray tea in hand.

"Exactly. I knew you would know him." Sam pats my knee, satisfied with my guess.

"Wow! He's hot."

"I know. He used to model. Calvin Klein. Underwear. But then he threw away that amazing op to go to law school." He makes a face.

"Could be worse."

"True. He could study philosophy or English Literature or something pointless."

"Better to be qualified than happy."

"Exactly." He nods, my sarcasm lost on him. "Where's Kristen? I need you girls to help me decide on my ensemble for my date."

"She's on her way back. When is your date and where are you going?"

"Tonight. Santelli's Ristorante."

"Damn. I heard Santelli's is crazy exclusive."

"I know." Sam bounces on my bed, his glasses dancing down his nose. "So, how's Cade? I overheard someone in the cafeteria talking about the announcement of his cancer on ESPN. That must suck to have it broadcasted."

"What? They announced it?"

Sam nods.

"What the hell? Cade hasn't released a statement yet. That must have blindsided him. How did they even confirm it? What did they say?"

"Do I look like someone who watches ESPN for news?"

"I hope Cade hasn't seen it yet. Maybe Miers will give him a heads-up that the information leaked so he isn't caught off guard. Or worse, put on the spot."

"How's he doing?"

"I don't know." I sigh. "He's avoiding me. Kind of. He had Miers message me that he's home and talking to his parents. I don't know how to read him. I feel like I'm just stumbling through it all with him."

"I'm sure it's better than him stumbling alone."

"Maybe."

"Trust me, if he didn't want you around, he would tell you."

"Thanks, Sam."

"No worries." He pats my knee again, oblivious.

"Oh good, you're here too." Kristen walks through the door, picking up the spare glass of wine from my bedside table. She downs it in three large gulps. "I have a date."

"Me too!" Sam gushes, jumping off the bed and taking Kristen's hands in his.

"When?" They ask each other in unison.

"Tonight!"

"Ahhhhh!"

Rolling my eyes at their being so damn extra, I can't help but smile.

"Let's get ready together. Go get your outfit options so I can veto the ones that suck," Kristen tells Sam.

"Okay, I'll be right back." He darts out of our bedroom.

"I'm so glad you're here." She hugs me. "I'm super nervous."

"Who are you going out with?"

"Joe Miers. Cade's friend."

"What?" My mouth drops open in surprise. I totally did not see that coming.

"Can you believe he asked me out?"

I roll my eyes. Kristen has no idea how mesmerizing she is. "Of course I can. Now let's make you look irresistible and downright smashing, dahling!"

Kristen giggles as I refill her glass.

Jealousy, that green-eyed bitch, infiltrates my relief as I take in my friend's glowing eyes and bright smile. Sam returns with a stack of clothing, his voice several octaves higher than usual.

It's messed up and I hate myself for it, but I wish I was going on a date tonight too.

21

CADE

"You ready?" Lila's voice surprises me as she leans against my F150, one foot kicked up behind her on the running board.

"What're you doing here?"

"You're starting chemo."

"I know that. What I don't understand is… why are you here?"

She winces and I hate that I sound like a dick. But I don't know what to expect today and the last thing I need is her witnessing me fall apart.

Slipping on a mask to hide her hurt, she opens her hand. "I'm coming to keep you company. Give me your keys."

"Lila."

"Keys, Cade." Her voice is stern, no nonsense, and I find myself enjoying this side of her even though I don't want to. I don't want to enjoy her anymore because it's going to hurt that much more when I'm forced to give her up. Our days are numbered. Now I just need to grow a pair and tell her.

Staring at her bold, unapologetic eyes, the firmness of her lips, I sigh. I need to pick my battles and ending things with

Lila, even if it's for her own good, isn't going to help me get through chemo today.

"I'll drive there. You can drive home," I compromise.

She nods once and walks to the passenger side of the truck. We drive to the hospital mostly in silence. Lila attempts small talk once or twice, but I shut it down. My head is all over the place and I don't want to take my dark thoughts out on her.

When we arrive at the hospital, I shoulder the bag I packed. She places her tiny hand in mine, and I squeeze gently. A silent thank-you. As much as I don't want to need her, in this moment, I do. And I'm relieved I'm not doing this alone.

Registering at reception, I'm escorted to meet my oncology nurse, Amanda. She runs me through the plan for today: a brief physical check, a blood sample, the chemo. Handing over a stack of papers to read and sign, my gratitude spikes when Lila accepts them on my behalf, sticking them into her shoulder bag.

Is that the same bag from the airport? Jesus, was that really only a few months ago? And now we're here, at an appointment for chemotherapy.

Within the hour, I'm sitting in a comfortable chair, an IV connected to the central venous catheter the doctors implanted into my chest before I left the hospital, being pumped with chemo. Lila reads her Kindle as I catch up on homework. But I can't concentrate on the words. After re-reading the same paragraph for the fifth time I snap the book shut.

Leaning forward, I take the stack of medical papers and Osteosarcoma literature from Lila's bag, but she stops me. "We can read that another time. I have a better idea."

"Really?"

She rummages in her bag and removes a deck of cards and a plastic bag of quarters. "You think you can beat me?"

"Texas hold 'em?"

"I'd play you for clothes." She glances around surreptitiously. "But we might get kicked out, and I can't have that on my conscience."

Touched by her thoughtfulness, a fault line ripples through my chest in warning. *Don't lead her on. Don't get too attached. You have to let her go.*

But it's going to kill me.

If cancer doesn't first.

"We'll have to play for quarters," she continues, emptying the baggie of change onto a side table and dividing it in half. She shuffles the cards expertly. "Ready?"

"Yeah. You're going down, Avers."

"We'll see about that."

"Yo, DUDE. YOU OKAY?" Miers's voice is quiet. "Come on, man. Let's get you up." His hands are surprisingly gentle on my back. They feel cool against my forehead. "Shit, dude. I think you got a fever."

His hands shift under my armpits as he tries to lift me. I struggle to get my feet underneath me, but my legs don't cooperate and I hang like dead weight in his arms. "I'll be back in a minute." He lays me on my side.

The tiles of the bathroom floor are cold against my skin, reminding me of the hangovers I would nurse in high school. In my head, I chuckle at the memory, but it floats away before I can laugh aloud.

"Okay, you get his left side," Miers instructs.

"You're okay, thirty-three." Hendrix is here.

The two of them hoist me up and half carry, half drag me into my room. They lay me on my bed and Miers disappears while Hendrix pours a cup of water. "Take small sips." He holds the cup to my mouth.

When Miers returns, he runs a damp cloth over my face and neck. Is he cleaning up my puke? Oh God, why? This is so embarrassing. Disgusting. But I'm tired. Too tired to be mortified. Too tired to care. All I feel is a twinge of relief that it's Miers and Hendrix, not Lila, cleaning me up and putting me to bed.

Wisps of sleep float around the corners of my mind, pulling my memories into dreams. My eyelids close.

"Sleep on your side, Wilkins." Hendrix shifts my weight.

I open my mouth to thank him, but I'm not sure if I do.

When I wake up, tiny hands rest on top of my head, fingers drawing figure-eights through my hair.

"Shh." Lila hushes my attempts to speak. "Just close your eyes and rest."

Folding her hand in mine, I press all the things I can't say into her skin.

Thank you.

I'm sorry.

I'm scared.

I love you. So damn much.

But you deserve better than this.

22

LILA

Cracking my first smile this week, I answer Mia's FaceTime call.

"Ciao bella!"

"Ciao Li. How are you? Maura told me about Cade."

"Real talk? I'm a mess." I rake my teeth over my bottom lip.

"What's going on?"

"A lot."

"Talk."

"I'm scared if I start it's going to be word vomit."

"Puke away." Mia leans closer, her chocolate eyes solemn.

Sighing, I open my mouth, and all the word vomit falls out. "I'm so worried about him. The chemo is affecting more than just his body. He's struggling mentally because his body isn't physically doing what he expects it to. He's embarrassed around me every time he gets sick which obviously, is a lot. He's angry with himself for feeling tired. It's just, it's a lot. And things between us are strained. He doesn't call me

"Lovely" anymore or tell me that he loves me. It's like I annoy him now," I admit, relieved to say all the things I'm feeling out loud. Somehow, saying them absolves me from the guilt I feel for thinking them.

"It would be a lot for anyone, at any time, to handle. It must be pure hell for him. He's probably devastated about football and his future. Feeling sick on top of everything would mess with anyone's head."

"I don't know what to do around him. How do I support him without it seeming like pity?" I raise a hand to my face and scrub my fingers across my eyes. "His friends called me the other night after he spiked a fever and I went over. It was awful, Mia." I shudder, remembering Cade's lifeless form, the exhaustion and despair that clung to his frame like cellophane wrap. "This is my own fault. I proposed the pact, wanted us to push past our comfort zones and live in the present. Now reality is knocking me flat on my ass."

"Give him some time to come to terms with everything. And if he starts to wallow too long, that's when you step in with some tough love. Like you guys did for me." She raises her eyebrows, giving me a stern look.

"I remember," I admit, hating when Maura, Emma, and I had to snap Mia out of her funk after a knee injury dashed her ballerina dreams.

"Like I think we're going to have to do with Maura soon."

Mia's sentence pulls me back to the present. "What? What's going on with her?"

Mia holds her finger up to me, speaking in rapid Italian to someone in the next room. "Sorry, I have to go. I promise, we'll talk more soon. For now, just be there for Cade, whatever he needs. And keep acting like yourself. If you treat him differently than you did before his diagnosis, you'll only make him feel worse."

"Yeah, that makes sense."

"Hang in there, Li."

"'Bye, Mia."

Gah. When did everything become so complicated? So damn convoluted? I can still hear the four of us girls laughing, huddled around the café table and eating pizza the night before Mia left for Rome. We made the college pact, which at the time I thought was genius, and here we are, handling serious issues and real problems.

I'm such an idiot.

"Oh good! You're here." Kristen waltzes into our dorm room, Sam close behind her.

"What's up?"

"Hey." Sam kisses my cheek in greeting before flopping next to me on my bed. "How come you didn't tell us you enrolled in the MCAT prep course?"

"Ugh. My dad signed me up."

"Without asking you?" Kristen looks up from where she's sifting through notebooks on her desk.

"Yeah. It's the worst timing ever. I don't know how I'm going to spend any time with Cade now."

"Has this internship clarified your future plans at all?" Kristen presses.

I shrug, falling back until my head hits my mattress. *Say it, Lila. Tell them.*

"I know your dad is putting a lot of pressure on you but it's nice he at least knows things about the medical school process. Like, we're supposed to enroll in a prep course this semester," Kristen says. "I wonder if my parents even know I have to take a qualifying exam for med school?"

"Everyone knows that." Sam turns his head toward mine,

staring at my profile. "Lila, it's better to take the prep course now. You'll be ahead of the curve. And if you decide to apply to some elite program, you won't have to scramble to prepare for the test at the last minute."

"I don't want to apply to med school." I blink at the ceiling. "Last week, I sat outside the hospital's main entrance. I watched as patients and doctors and families walked in and out of the main doors. And do you know what I felt?"

"What?" Sam rolls onto his side, peering into my face.

"Relieved that my shift was over. I don't want to do the twelve-hour shifts. I don't want to deal with the warring emotions of losing a patient, of having to tell the family. I don't want to balance the enormity of being a good healer in addition to being a good girlfriend, friend, and person. I just, I don't want it."

"Are you sure? Or is this because of Cade?"

"What? No, of course not."

"No one would blame you if you had second thoughts now that your boyfriend is experiencing well, what he's experiencing."

Kristen abandons her desk and drops down on my other side. "It's your dad, isn't it?"

"Ding, ding, ding. Winner."

"You need to talk to him. It's fine to change your mind. That's why people even go to college these days, to figure out what they want to pursue next. Just tell him now before he starts sending you Harvard Medical School hoodies." Kristen picks my phone up and hands it to me.

A hoodie would be the icing on the cake. "I need to call him."

"We'll give you a few minutes." Kristen stands, giving Sam a look until he follows her from our room.

"She's going to call him now?" Sam whispers to Kristen as the door closes behind them.

Should I wait until tomorrow? Or next semester?

He's busy.

He could be in a meeting.

Or with Brenda.

Kristen pops her head around our dorm room door. "I don't hear you talking."

"I don't know what to say," I admit, throwing myself against my mattress again.

"How about the truth?"

"But I'm not sure what I want to do. It's not like I have some great passion that I want to focus on instead. I've never given this any real thought. I just always followed along, got A's in the science courses, and figured why not become a doctor?"

Kristen narrows her eyes at me like she doesn't understand. She sighs heavily. "Okay, what other interests do you have?"

I shrug, which is a lot harder to pull off when one is lying sprawled across a bed like a damsel in distress.

"Give me something to work with here."

I sit back up. "I want to help people."

"Okay, there are tons of professions in the medical field that don't require you to become a doctor. You don't have to start over because you majored in biology. You can pursue research."

"Ew."

"Or look into physician assistant programs. You can check out hospital administration. Physical or occupational therapy."

"They're all options." I drag my toe across the carpet.

"Call your dad. It's like ripping off a Band-Aid." She nods curtly, stepping back into the hallway and closing the door.

"Or cutting your own throat," I say to no one, selecting Dad in my contact list and pressing send.

It rings twice before his voice comes through the line. "Hey, Li."

"Hi, Dad."

"How's the MCAT prep course going?"

Not the start I was going to lead with but okay. "It's going."

"I spoke with Joe Richardson at UMass last week. He sent me information on their medical program. I'll forward it to you. UMass could be a good fit for you."

FML. "Great. Thanks."

"How's the internship? Did you read my e-mail? Did you make an appointment to speak with Kate Lenox yet? She has a lot of contacts she can connect you with."

"Not yet."

He sighs and I can picture him removing his glasses, setting them down on his desk, and rubbing his eyes the way he does when he's exasperated. Clearly, I exasperate him. "You really need to get on the ball, Lila. This is a wonderful opportunity and you shouldn't throw it away. Get your head out of the bottle and stay away from the tailgates and focus on what's important, sweetheart. On things that matter."

Like family? My throat burns with the unspoken words. "Okay, Dad," I grind out instead.

"Okay. Well, sweetheart, as happy as I am to hear from you, I'm at the golf course and tee off is in five."

Really? "Good luck with that."

"Study hard now and make me proud. Bye, Lila."

I hang up the phone and flop back down across the bed, draping my arm over my eyes.

That was an epic fail.

Kristen walks back in the room, Sam close behind her, and fixes me with a glare. "You suck."

"I know."

NOVEMBER

23

CADE

"Game day, dude." Miers bangs his fist on my doorjamb, entering my room.

"Victory is ours," I mutter.

"Your enthusiasm is contagious."

"Fuck off. Don't you think riding the bench seems masochistic?"

"You heard Coach. Being a leader means leading by example."

I groan, scrubbing a hand over my face. "Who knew cancer could be so inspirational?"

"Aw, come on. Don't pull the cancer card." Miers drops into my desk chair, stacking his feet on the edge of my bed.

"Can I help you with something?"

"Dude, where's Lila been at?"

"What do you mean?" I sit up in bed, my comforter pooling around my hips.

"Is she ghosting you? Or are you pushing her out of your life one snide comment at a time?"

"This isn't how I want to start my day."

"Yeah, well, me either. But dude, don't screw up the best part of your life right now."

"It's complicated."

"Only because you're making it that way." Miers stands, shuffling to the door. "I'll save you a plate for breakfast. See you at the game?"

"I'll be there," I grumble, laying back down after Miers leaves.

On some irritating level, I know he's right. I am pushing Lila away. Or maybe she's pulling away? Whatever, it doesn't matter. What does matter is that there is distance between us now and I can't seem to move past it. I don't want her to see me falling apart after every chemo session. I don't want her pity. Don't want to witness the heartbreak in her eyes when I can't pull myself up off the bathroom floor.

I know Lila and I need to talk, to have a real conversation, but for some selfish, fucked up reason, I'm still holding on to a sliver of hope that things between us will shift. That I'll magically heal and be able to have the future with her that I want.

That I can allow myself to need her as much as I want to.

By the time I drag myself downstairs, the house is empty. The aroma of crisp bacon and fluffy waffles floats throughout the first floor as I enter the kitchen.

A foil-covered plate sits on the counter with a note in Hendrix's writing.

Thirty-Three – Happy you're coming to the game today. Make sure you eat good grub before kick-off.

Uncovering the plate, I grin at the heap of pancakes, side of scrambled eggs, slightly burnt bacon, and whole-wheat bagel smeared in peanut butter. Pouring myself a mug of coffee, I sit down. Even though I'm not hungry, I force myself to eat the breakfast of champions.

WATCHING a football game from the sidelines is strange. Dusk falls quickly and the day disappears, leaving behind a cool breeze and the rustle of leaves. The stadium is lit up by the nightlights. Fans cheer loudly, holding up signs and shaking banners, honking noisemakers, participating in The Wave as it circulates the stadium. The band beats steadily on drums, and cheerleaders fly through the night sky.

Game day always carries an alluring charm, suspending the team between reality and an otherworldly phenomenon. It's like we have the ability to transform, for a few short hours, from regular football players into warriors. I've always reveled in the sacredness that is football. As I watch the Mustangs line up for kick-off, gratefulness floods my chest to still experience moments like this, days like today, and the spirit of the game.

My eyes are glued to the field, drinking in each flawless pass, applauding every catch, shouting when the Mustangs score. Recalling the experience of racing down the field, rolling across a yard-line to achieve a first-down, kneeling in the end zone, my past humbles me and forces me to appreciate the opportunity I had to lead a team like the Mustangs. Watching them seize their victory tonight is an honor.

When the team rushes the bench after the game, I'm swept into the huddle, the wild whooping, the backslapping, the whistles and helmet smacking. For a moment, I almost feel like myself.

Me: *Hey, I can't make the game today.*
  Cade: OK. See you after?
Me: Yes. I'll come by later tonight. Movie?
Cade: Sure. See you then.

Cade and I are a sinking ship. Every exchange is strained. Each interaction teems with tension, of the awkward variety. There's a wall between us that I don't know how to break down or climb over and it hurts me just as much as it pisses me off. Why doesn't anyone warn you that adulting is so freaking hard?

I should be at Cade's football game now, supporting him while he sits on the bench and watches his team advance without his leadership. But the impending conversation with my dad is hanging over my head like an anvil. I need to rip off the Band-Aid and start making adult decisions about my future.

Squeezing my eyes shut, I call Dad.

"Lila," he answers.

"Hey, Dad. How are you?"

"Fine, sweetheart. And you?"

"Do you have a minute? There's something I want to run by you."

"Sure. Is this something about your meeting with Kate Lenox? I'm assuming you've spoken with her. Do you like the program at UMass?"

Jeez. He just doesn't let up. "No. Actually, I haven't spoken with Mrs. Lenox or checked out the program at UMass." *Deep breath. I can do this.* "I don't think, no, I know that I don't want to attend medical school."

Silence.

"Lila…" long sigh "…I know you're angry with me. But, sweetheart, don't make a huge mistake just to spite me. You're better than this. Make the appointment with Kate Lenox, continue the MCAT course, and next semester you'll thank me for not allowing you to quit."

Allowing me? Thanking him! "Dad, you're not hearing what I'm saying. I don't want to apply to medical school. I'm not sure what I want to do yet, but this isn't it. I've learned a lot during this internship, mainly that this isn't the career or future that I want. I'm not doing this to anger you or out of spite or anything like that. I'm not applying to medical school because I don't want to be a doctor."

Opening my eyes, I clutch the phone in my hand. Whoa, lightness rolls through me, the weight subsiding.

Except Dad hasn't responded.

Dread creeps back in, pulling me under like quicksand. "Dad?"

"I didn't expect this from you. With Brandon, he didn't have your grades so a part of me understood his reluctance, his fear of rejection. He wouldn't have been able to handle the pressure. But you've always been so smart, ambitious, and levelheaded. I never imagined that one semester in California, playing house with a football player, would make you forfeit your dreams. What are you going to do? Follow this boy around? Nurse him back to health like a maid when you could be saving lives like a doctor?"

"This has nothing to do with Cade." *Don't give him the satisfaction of knowing his words affect me.*

"Whatever you tell yourself at night, sweetheart. I am so disappointed in you. Good luck figuring out what to do next. You graduate in May. Who is going to hire a giggly girl with no technical skills and no idea what to do with her life? And if you think I'm going to keep supporting you, paying for your lush lifestyle, you are mistaken. Call me back when you wake up." He disconnects.

Shock slices through me at the venom in his words. Rolling my shoulders forward, I drop into my desk chair, unseeing. His words landed like rocks and something deep inside shatters. A fog wraps around my brain as I try, again and again, to make sense of his response.

But I can't. Because it's hateful and bitter and hurtful.

I'm not enough for him. He cares more about the doctor title than he does about my feelings, my thoughts, my happiness. Me.

Now what do I do?

What does my future look like without all the plans and deadlines? What is my purpose?

Questions ping-pong around my brain and shame flares to life, lighting a fire to combat the cold in my blood. But I don't have any answers.

Not even one.

Opening my laptop, I type out an email.

To: amelia.petrella@mcshain.edu, emma.stanton@mcshain.edu, maura.rodriguez@mcshain.edu

From: lila.avers@mcshain.edu

Date: November 4, 2015
Subject: Life Decisions
Hi friends,

I miss you girls. I've made some important life decisions – i.e. I'm not applying to medical school. And my dad lost it. He didn't lose it in the way I expected – there was no yelling or hollering. It was worse. He was cold, disconnected, and disappointed. I'm so angry/upset/frustrated I could scream. I mean, is it really that horrible if his daughter doesn't want to be a doctor? There are a lot of other things I could do, right?

Do you have any ideas on what they could be?

I am so confused and lost right now. Like I'm going through the motions of this internship that so many students are desperate to be a part of, and my heart's not in it. And then I feel guilty because I should be grateful to have been accepted in the first place and to not struggle with the demanding academic load like so many other people. Sigh, I'm a mess.

On top of that, Cade and I aren't connecting. Some days we're good but most days, everything is awful. I want to be here for him, but I don't always know how to do that without him becoming defensive or feeling like I pity him. Maybe I do pity him a little? I mean, I know I feel terrible for him. But I don't see him any differently. I'm still incredibly attracted to him (you girls have seen his photos – he's sexy AF). He makes me laugh and he makes me feel so many things I've never experienced before. But it's different now. Maybe because we can't act on the physical attraction part? He's so tired all the time and lost in his own head.

What do you guys think I should do?

Write soon with updates.

Missing you all.

25

CADE

"I brought popcorn." Lila holds up a box of Orville Redenbacher popcorn for our movie night.

"Come on in."

The tension between us is palpable, an undercurrent of frustration and pressure, that we continue to ignore. Tonight marks the third Saturday that she has hung in with me, watched old movies stretched across my bed and munched on popcorn, instead of joining her friends for drinks, dancing on tables, and barhopping like most college seniors.

And I hate it. Guilt clogs my veins like plaque, spreading slowly. I'm scared when it finally erupts, it will be like a heart-attack. One that ends us with no chance of recovery.

"We should talk," I start but she lifts a finger to indicate she needs a minute as she reads a text message, a small laugh filling the silence between us.

"Hm?" she asks after a minute. "Want to watch a comedy or a drama?" Flopping down on my bed, she scrolls through Netflix options.

"It doesn't matter."

"Okay." She settles on an episode of *New Girl*, her atten

Love,
Lila

tion diverted to another chime from her phone. Her fingers fly across the keypad as she taps out a reply.

After the fifth message, I'm restless, more focused on the texts lighting up her phone screen than I am on Zooey Deschanel. Shifting my weight, I bump my leg against hers until she loses the faraway look in her eyes, places her phone down, and turns to me.

"You okay?" she asks, oblivious to my mounting frustration.

"Are you?"

"What do you mean?"

"You've been messaging all night. Something important going on? Something you don't want to miss out on but are because you're stuck hanging with me?"

Her eyes narrow, anger slanting the corners sharply. "What are you talking about?"

"You're completely distracted. I get that you don't want to be here. And that's fine. I wouldn't want to be here either if I was you. So why don't you just go, meet up with Kristen and Sam, and do whatever it is you'd rather be doing?"

Her face contorts, confusion, hurt, and then anger flashing in her irises. "Are you kidding me right now?" She turns her body toward mine, her tone accusatory when she spits out, "Am I not supposed to have friends or a life outside of you?"

"Of course you are! That's my point. You're *supposed* to be enjoying your senior year. You're *supposed* to be going to parties with your friends. You're *supposed* to be having fun. Instead, you're cooped up in a house with a bunch of football players playing caretaker to an invalid."

"Oh that's mature. Degrade yourself."

"Lila, look around you. We're watching *New Girl* for the third Saturday night in a row. Wait, last weekend it was *Modern Family*. You're wasting your time with me. I'm letting you off the hook. I know it must be tough to tell the guy with cancer that this just isn't for you, but really, it's not for anyone. And I can't keep doing this. So please, leave and meet up with whoever keeps messaging you."

"You want me to go? Are you, what, breaking up with me?"

"I'm giving you back your life. I'm giving you a choice."

"Really? It seems like you've already made my choice for me. What is it with men?"

"Men? What are you talking about?" Is she involved with someone else? Rage blinds me, a jealousy that's almost violent in its intensity, consumes my ability to think rationally. What men?

"Men! My dad thinking he can just dictate my future for me, you thinking you can just dole out my weekend activities, like playdates for a three-year-old. Why does everyone think I'm incapable of living my own life? Making my own decisions?"

"What are you talking about with your dad?" My tone is calmer, my jealousy doused in a bucket of cold water. After our first date eating Italian ice, Lila's barely mentioned her family. Her raising the subject now piques my curiosity. Is this why she's been so distant lately? Have I been too self-absorbed to realize that she's going through things too?

"I'm not applying to medical school."

"What are you talking about? That's the whole reason you're here."

"Wow, thanks for that enlightening observation. My being here, my internship, made me realize that I don't want to be a doctor so I'm not going to apply."

"Lila, wait." My arm snakes out, my hand closing around her wrist. "That doesn't make any sense. What are you even talking about?"

"You sound just like him," she tsks, disappointment coloring her tone. I imagine she's referring to her father, which pisses me off.

"You just blindsided me. I don't understand why you would make such a drastic decision. Is it because of me? You can't do this just because I have cancer."

Cue eye roll. "No, Cade, it's not because of you. I've been feeling this way for a really long time. It just, it all finally came to a head between my Dad and me. That's all."

"You've been feeling this way for a long time? Why didn't you tell me?"

"Because I was figuring things out."

"And you didn't think to discuss your future with me? Or your thoughts about it?"

"You have a lot of other things to focus on."

I bark out a humorless laugh. "That's right, because I have cancer. So that means, I'm completely useless and can't be included in my own damn relationship."

"Don't put words in my mouth, Cocky."

"Don't make decisions without consulting me, Lila."

"Consulting you?" She jumps up, her eyes wide, wild. "I don't owe you anything, Cade. This is my decision. It has nothing to do with you."

"Why? Because you're not planning on sticking around? Because you already know that we don't have a chance in hell at making this work?"

"Stop putting words in my mouth. I can articulate myself just fine without you making assumptions."

"It's not making an assumption when it's so damn obvious that right now, you'd rather be somewhere else. So decide, are you staying or are you going?" I slam my fist against my chest before pointing toward the door, my anger spiking to a whole new level because that hurt.

Lila stands from my bed, her posture ready to pounce. Her eyes turn arctic as she glares at me. Raising a finger, she jabs it in the air. "Don't make this about me. What do you want? Do you really want me to leave? Are you so embarrassed to need help, to need a support system, that you're willing to just toss me aside?"

Her words squeeze around my heart until little fissures form, cracking it. I need to end this now. If I don't, she'll keep at it. She'll waste her entire senior year, her whole future, and for what? "I think it's for the best if we take a break. Focus on you, your future, your life. And I'll focus on mine."

Unexpected laughter bursts from her mouth, her cheeks blazing. "A break?"

"Yeah."

"Screw you, Cade." Her eyes shine with tears for a moment before she blinks, hardens herself against the pain I'm causing her. Then she gathers her purse and storms out of my bedroom.

And I let her go.

26

LILA

"Is he fucking kidding me? Making decisions for me like I'm a child? Giving me choices?"

Dashing from Cade's house, I run to Kristen's car around the corner, the night breeze doing nothing to soothe the heat rippling off my skin. Clenching my fingers into fists, I bang them down on the hood of Kristen's car, screaming out into the dark, as hot tears pool in the corners of my eyes.

Cade broke up with me.

We're over.

Doubling over, pain grips my stomach, twisting my intestines. *Oh God, I'm going to be sick.* Bile rises in my throat and I swallow it back, sinking to the curb. Hanging my head, tears fall from my eyes into my cupped palms, mixing with the snot dripping from my nose.

Sucking in a breath, a screech mixed with a groan rings out.

It's me. I sound like a deer that's been shot.

I can't do this. I can't breathe. Cade broke up with me.

And it hurts. Oh God, it hurts.

Forcing myself to relocate to Kristen's car, I slam the door closed and drop my head to the steering wheel. I choke on the anguished sobs that wrack my body, splitting my chest like shifting tectonic plates. Fisting my fingers into my eyes, I try to halt my tears, but they keep coming, like a sudden collapse of the Hoover Dam. My emotions overwhelm me, leaving me drained, as the events from today – my conversation with my dad, my decision not to apply to medical school, my break with Cade – level me.

I'm ugly crying. This is ugly crying.

That's what Maura calls it. The big, heaving sobs that originate from the center of your being, making you feel like you're breaking from the inside out. My eyelids swell from the torrent of tears and I'm forced to breathe through my mouth to avoid choking on my own tears.

Ugly crying.

I nearly laugh thinking about Maura and how she begged us to give her a free pass for all her ugly-crying last semester. Right now, I wish she was sitting in the seat next to me, passing me tissues and rattling off quips to make me smile.

Loneliness wraps around me, deepening my sadness, highlighting the disconnect I feel. I miss my friends. I miss home.

Gradually, my tears subside. My eyelids droop and my head throbs, beating in time with my slowing pulse. The silence reassures me, the night sky providing a sliver of comfort.

Checking my phone, I see four missed calls from Cade, two from Kristen, one from Sam. A stream of messages fills my inbox, all with various sayings like "call me" and "are you okay?" and "where are you?"

Gah! As much as I don't want Kristen and Sam to see me

like this, I also don't want to sleep in Kristen's car like a homeless person and avoid everyone I know.

Ignoring all of Cade's messages, I respond to Kristen and Sam in a group text.

Me: Hey. What are you guys doing tonight? I'm down for going out.

Their responses are immediate.

Kristen: Ahh, glad to hear from you. Going to a party on Elm Street. Come! It will be fun. xx

Sam: Are you okay? Going to a party on Elm. Should be a good time. Come through. I'll carry your drunk ass home.

Me: See you there.

A party sounds like the perfect setting to glue some of my broken heart back together and forget for a while. Today was shit and I want a distraction more than I want to wallow.

Pulling my makeup bag out of my purse, I flick on the overhead light in Kristen's car. Digging out my bronzer and blush, I try to conceal the tear tracks that mark my cheeks. My eyelids are still puffy but look considerably better after a few swipes of mascara. Maybe I should focus on my lips since they actually look sexy in a bee-stung sort of way. I line them and add a lip tint and gloss.

Next, I turn to my hair, running a comb through it and braiding the front pieces back. Pinning them in place with bobby pins I find scattered at the bottom of my purse, I evaluate my look. Not my best, but not tragic either.

Popping Kristen's trunk, I rummage through the random clothes and shoes she stores there in case of an emergency. Smart girl. I'll have to thank her later. And tell Emma that we need to do this starting now until forever. Settling on a short, tight navy dress and a pair of nude pumps, I change in the backseat of the car.

Taking a fortifying breath, I steel my spine, some of my nerves settling.

Fuck men and their stupid meddling.

I don't need anyone but myself.

And tonight, I'm ready to forget all about today.

27

CADE

"Fuck." I start into the hallway as Lila slams the front door closed.

"Slow your roll, thirty-three," Miers's voice is calm but his grip on my shoulder is strong.

Shaking him off, I turn and glare. "What the hell?"

"Let her go, dude. She needs some space."

"You don't even know what happened."

"I know that when a girl takes off like that, she needs to cool down. Anything you say to her right now is going to add fuel to whatever fire you guys are burning. If you want to have a real conversation, a constructive conversation, let her calm down a bit."

Pinching the bridge of my nose, I know he's right. She needs time. She needs space. Still, the way her eyes shone with unshed tears slices through me, and I hate myself for causing her to doubt me, to question us.

"I'm doing this for her own good. I only want what's best for her." Which, right now, is obviously not me. I wouldn't even be good for a goldfish in my current state: sick, bitter, weak, depressed.

"If you say so, dude."

What the hell was I thinking picking a fight with her when she made an important life decision today? And why did I assume it was about me? Why do I keep assuming that everything is about me?

I shake my head at Miers as he turns to follow me back to my bedroom. I need time, space, a minute to be alone.

And mourn the girl who ran out the front door with my heart clutched in her hands.

REGRET.

It seeps deeper into my bones and fills up the cracks in my chest the more time passes without hearing from Lila.

Regret.

Damn, did I handle everything wrong? My words were harsh, my delivery cruel. Learning that she made so many life decisions without confiding in me scraped at my nerves, caused a flare of anger to erupt when I should have shown her empathy.

So I call her. Several times. And she doesn't answer any of them.

The more minutes that pass, the more desperate I become. Did she make it home okay? Did she meet up with Kristen and Sam? Are they drowning her sorrows in margaritas and having a bitch fest about the biggest douchebag they know?

When my phone beeps, I trip over my own feet lunging for it.

Miers: I'm breaking relationship code and abiding by bro code. Kristen heard from Lila. She's meeting her at that party on Elm Street. I promised to be DD so no worries, dude, I'll make sure she gets home in one piece.

Good. As much as I want Lila to enjoy her senior year and have fun with her friends, I don't want her to blaze a path of recklessness just because she's pissed at me. Jesus, what if she hooks up with someone tonight?

Speaking from experience, I know how angry girls react when you tell them something they don't want to hear. They go for the jugular, do something to make you jealous, make you react. They get all sexified with their girls for a night of drinking and debauchery.

In the past, I never cared. But this time, I would react. Clenching my hands into fists, my thoughts jump to the worst-case scenarios; I already am reacting.

Please, Lila, don't hook up with a random.

Me: Miers, are you going to this party with Kristen?

Miers: Swinging by later on. Figured the girls could do their thing for a bit. Why? You want to come?

Because I know him so well, I know that he's goading me. He knows that I don't want any guys posting up on Lila.

Me: Yeah. I'll come with you, bro. Let me know when you head out.

Miers: Yep, I'll hit you up later on. Getting dinner with K now.

Tossing my phone aside, I close my eyes. I've officially gone from being the life of the party to needing life injections to make it to the party.

28

LILA

The Elm Street party is popping when I roll up. I feel strange going to a party alone but remind myself that this is what single girls do, they take life by the balls and throw themselves into the midst of it. I can do this. I mean, I was single just a few months ago. I know it's the rejection clinging to my insides, making me question myself.

But damn, I used to be fearless, badass, a social freaking butterfly.

All I need to do is feign confidence until I'm tipsy enough not to care about how I act. Twinges of doubt are nothing a little liquid courage can't fix.

The music is loud, pouring out of the open windows and spilling from the porch, mingling with the shouts and laughter of drunken college students. Ah, senior year. I may actually miss this: the smell of stale beer, the wide-eyed glazed-over look of stoners, the infectious giggle of drunken sorority girls.

Tugging the bottom of Kristen's dress down as I walk up the stairs of the porch, I release my breath and stop fiddling with the hem. Who am I kidding? I have great legs. Big deal if the dress rides up.

I'm single, right?

Raising my head with faux confidence, I scrunch the roots of my hair for some volume and walk through the front doors like I am the party.

Beelining to the bar, I eye up the four guys hanging there. Excellent. "Anyone want to take a shot with me?"

Four sets of eyes swivel in my direction, caressing my body lazily, checking out the goods.

I haven't flirted in ages.

Cocking my head to the side, I raise my eyebrows.

One of the guys pours five shots of tequila and pushes one in my direction. "I'd love to, sweetheart."

"Bottoms up." I raise my shot. The liquid burns a path down my throat, warming the chill in my chest, thawing the frozen block where my heart used to beat.

I'm four shots and two drinks in when Kristen walks through the front door, Sam behind her.

"Hey, bitches!" I yell at them, swatting away a guy's hand on my ass. "'Bout time you got here."

"Look at you." Sam twirls me, tossing an arm over my shoulder. He says something to Kristen over my head, but I don't make out the words. "Let's grab some beers." Sam maneuvers me to the bar, handing me a bottle of water.

Shaking my head, I pull Kristen to the makeshift dance floor. "I love this song!" I sway, grinding my hips to the music and grinning at the appreciative whistles that break out around me, laughing at whoever smacks my ass.

"Li, are you okay?"

"I'm great! Dance with me?"

"What happened with Cade?"

"Kristen, not now. Just give me tonight. I need this." I gesture between us. "Friends, normal, a night out. Without talking or thinking about Cade Wilkins. Please?"

Her eyes soften as she looks me over. "Okay. Tonight, we party. Good times. Tomorrow, we discuss and rehash. Deal?"

"Deal!" I grab her hand and pull her back into the swell of pulsing bodies and swaying arms.

Losing myself in the music, I dance my ass off, grinding into the muscle that steps up behind me. When he wraps his arms around my waist, Kristen tries to pull me forward, out of his grasp, but I shake her off. The warmth of his hands, the musky scent of his cologne, the tickle of his breath on my shoulder, it's all wrong. And yet, it feels good, a reminder that I'm still good enough, still hot enough, for someone to want me. Closing my eyes to block out Kristen's expression, I enjoy the attention of a stranger.

Music pulses under my skin. The stale taste of cigarettes clouds my mind. My limbs feel disconnected from my body, like a jellyfish. Tonight, I'm carefree, light, floating on a marshmallow cloud of good times. The hands that press into my skin as I walk onto the patio for some air are like tiny nods of approval, boosting my confidence with their attention.

A guy offers me a cigarette and I accept even though I don't smoke. Not really. Exhaling, I watch the smoke curl and rise upwards, floating away. It's hazy and ethereal and delicate. It's beautiful. I reach out to touch it, but the wisps disappear, fading into the night sky.

"You okay?" Cigarette guy presses a hand into the small of my back, tugging me into his side.

I make a sound which he takes as confirmation to hold me closer, tighter.

Kristen will be looking for me. I was supposed to wait for her while she got me a bottle of water.

"What's your name?"

"Lila."

"I'm Tom." He attempts to shake my hand. A tattoo runs up the inside of his arm, partially hidden by the flannel sleeve that's cuffed to his mid forearm. It's a tribal tattoo, black ink. His forearms look strong, stable, sure. Cade's arms used to look like this. Cade has a tribal tattoo. It wraps around his ribcage and is insanely sexy when I drag my hands down his chest and around to his back. Thinking about Cade, I trace Tom's tattoo, running my fingertips up the inside of his arm. He inhales sharply but I'm too focused on the intricate pattern of his ink. Maybe I should get a tattoo?

"Are you having fun tonight?"

Of course I'm having fun. Can't he tell? I'm the life of the freaking party.

"Want a drink?" He holds out a Solo cup of something. I breathe it in. Rum.

Taking the cup from his hand, I tip it back, draining the liquid inside. "It's sweet."

"So are you."

I laugh.

His fingers are in my hair, tucking errant strands behind my ear. His touch is warm and comforting.

It's sweet.

29

CADE

"Dude, you're going to walk a hole through the carpet," Miers says, appearing in the doorway to my bedroom.

"She hasn't answered any of my messages. Not even the one just asking her to let me know she's safe, with her friends." *Damn, Lila. Did you have to turn out like every other girl I know? You got my attention, sweetheart.*

"Cade, give the girl some breathing room. You know she's safe and with Kristen and Sam."

Shaking my head, I bang my fist against the wall. "Something's off. I can't explain it but something's not right."

"Dude, you're just reeling because you broke up with your girl for being there for you."

"You're not helping."

"Come on, let's go get them. Then, you can see Lila and apologize for being a dick and hope she takes you back."

We're pulling out of the parking lot when Miers phone beeps. "Shit."

"What?"

"Kristen can't find Lila."

"What do you mean she can't find her?"

Miers jerks the gearstick into park so he can text with both hands.

We wait a few moments and the beep alerts us to a new message. I'm leaning over the center console trying to read what Kristen wrote. Maybe Lila went to the bathroom? Or she's with Sam? Or she was tired and went home without telling anyone? But even as these excuses run through my mind, I know they're not true.

Something is off. I can feel it.

"She can't find her. Kris went to get her a bottle of water and when she returned, Lila was gone. She's searching the house and asking everyone, but no one seems to know where she wandered off to. Sam is with Kristen." Miers fixes me with a level stare. "I'm sure she's fine."

"Drive."

Miers pushes the gearstick into drive and pulls out of the parking lot. I notice his foot is heavier than usual on the accelerator and my panic spikes.

Something is wrong.

Of course, because we are in such a hurry, we hit every single red light and get stuck behind every car driving below the speed limit. My knee jerks up and down and I can't stop my fingers from tapping out a rhythm on the side of the door.

When we arrive at Elm Street, sirens ring out. Students spill onto the front lawn, shoving each other as they try to leave the party. The red and blue lights of an ambulance flash in Miers's rearview mirror as we search for parking. The ambulance is parked in the driveway of the party house.

My stomach sinks.

30

LILA

Tom is dancing with me. His voice rasps in my ear, the stubble on his chin streaking across my shoulder. The sky is pulsing, the stars dancing to the beat of the music. In. Out. In. Out. They blink and wink and flicker. I reach out to touch one.

I STUMBLE ON A STEP, my wrist catching on the stairs, breaking my fall. Pain blooms, shooting up my arm. My bracelet gets stuck in the carpet but I'm quickly pulled upright, little strands of carpet clinging to the gold bangle.

HOT, rivulets of sweat drip down the center of my back. Perspiration dots my hairline. My clothes feel itchy, too tight, too heavy.

Why is it so hot in here?

A flash of red flannel followed by a sticky hand covering my mouth.

"Shh."

A tribal tattoo blocks out my vision.

MY BODY FEELS HEAVY, my arms won't lift and my legs won't move. Black dots and squiggly lines flash before my eyes. I want to touch one, hold on and pull myself up. But I can't. Hot hands rake over my body. Something rips in the quiet. My wrist pulses. The sky is dark and I don't see the stars.

Everything is a black void.

I'M WATCHING MYSELF, a total out-of-body experience. Red flannel moves above me, touching me, tasting the salty sweat from the skin of my neck, licking behind my ear. My dress hitches around my hips. My legs are limp. Where's my left shoe?

Clenching my hands into fists, I try to beat against the flannel but nothing happens. A scream dies in my throat. A flash of pain reverberates through my head and the left side of my face burns.

"Shh."

Panic freezes my chest. My mouth opens, but nothing comes out.

I can't breathe.

"LILA?" The voice at my side is gentle. It reminds me of my mother when I was small and sick. A cool hand presses against my forehead. Do I have the flu?

———

FLASHES of red and blue beat against the insides of my eyes, but I can't open them or ask the lights to go away. I can't move. I can't breathe. I can't.

31

CADE

"Sam!" Miers waves to catch Sam's attention as we cut across the lawn.

Sam turns, starting toward us. Pushing his glasses up higher on his nose, his characteristic gesture is forced, as if he doesn't know what to do with his hands so he's relying on habit. I've never seen him look so serious.

He shakes his head once, his eyes darting to the ambulance, indecision playing out over his features. And I know. I know without knowing that Lila is lying inside. That seconds later, when the ambulance backs out of the driveway, blares its sirens, and heads in the direction of the hospital, it's carrying Lila to the emergency room. It's Lila inside the ambulance and not some random freshman that drank too much and needs to get his stomach pumped.

"Where is she?"

"Cade." Sam's voice is strained.

"Where. Is. She?"

"She was in the ambulance."

Of course she was. "Who hurt her? What happened?"

"We need to get to the hospital." Miers's grip on my shoulder directs me toward his car.

My feet are already moving, pulling me back to the car, taking me one step closer to Lila.

She's hurt. She's hurt. She's hurt.

I need to see her. I need to be with her. And I need to be strong for her.

MIERS DRIVES quickly to the hospital. The air in the car is tense, strained, and it tastes stale when I breathe it in. Sam sits in the backseat, his elbows propped on his knees as he leans over the center console.

"I don't know. Kristen found her," he's saying in response to the rapid questions that Miers fires at him. My mind is too slow to think of anything to ask. All I know is that she's hurt.

"Did you see anything? Is she hurt?" Miers asks.

"Maybe a broken wrist. She has a cut on her forehead, through her eyebrow. And the left side of her face is starting to bruise," Sam continues.

"Did he …" Miers meets Sam's gaze in the rearview mirror, trailing off. But I know what he's asking. Was she raped?

"I don't know."

And suddenly I come back to the moment and react, punching my fist against Miers's glove box as hard as I can. The glove box dents and my hand throbs. Tense silence resumes. Sam leans back and Miers keeps his eyes on the road.

Pulling up to the hospital, Miers drops us off at the emergency entrance. Sam and I push through the doors and stumble to reception.

/ers," Sam snaps at the receptionist.

moment please. If you could just have a seat over the ne receptionist points at the waiting area, "someone will be with you shortly."

I want to punch the counter, but I hold back, turning sharply toward the waiting area and then continuing down the hallway. Sam lets me go.

I'm pacing the halls of the hospital.

Is she okay? I need to see her. Hold her. Comfort her. I need her.

When I enter the waiting area, I see Kristen sitting with Miers and Sam.

"Kristen." I launch forward, grabbing her wrist as I sink to the ground in front of her chair. "Tell me she's okay."

Kristen shakes her head, her eyes filling with tears. "The doctors are checking her for trauma. If she agrees, they'll do a rape kit."

I swear, bile rising in my throat. Fuck, what if Lila was raped?

"The doctors are testing her urine to see if she was drugged. Plus, they need to set her wrist..." Kristen continues but I can't focus on her words.

I need to have eyes on Lila. I need to see my lovely.

"I'm going to call her brother." Kristen stands and Miers shifts me into the vacant chair.

"Drink." Sam presses a coffee into my hand.

I raise it to my lips and take a large gulp, barely noticing as it scalds my throat.

32

LILA

"Lila?"

My eyelids flutter open and the light blinds me. Ugh. I feel sick. Like never-drinking-again sick.

Worst. Hangover. Ever.

"Lila?"

Turning my head, I lock eyes with Brandon.

"What are you doing here?" My voice is rough, raspy. Another raspy voice flickers through my mind but I shake my head, focusing on my brother. "Is Mom okay?"

"Mom's fine." Brandon leans forward, resting his elbows on his knees. He's half hunched over my bed. Except this isn't my bed. I take in the beeping machine to my right and the sound accelerates.

"Breathe. You're okay." Brandon squeezes my hand.

"What happened?"

He swallows and looks toward the door, briefly closing his eyes. "What do you remember?"

Remember? I think back to yesterday. Leaving Cade's house in a storm of anger. Rushing to Kristen's car. Crying hysterically. A party on Elm Street. Short blue dress.

Tequila shots, cigarettes. Dancing. Reaching out to touch a star.

"I went to a party."

Brandon nods encouragingly.

A red flannel shirt.

A tribal tattoo.

A raspy voice.

A black void.

Starless.

"Oh God."

Brandon stands up, shifting to the edge of my bed and enveloping me in his strong arms. "Shh." His hand runs over my hair. "You're okay. You were drugged. Some dick roofied you and tried to rape you."

Pulling back from his embrace, I look up, voicing my questions through my eyes so I don't have to speak them aloud.

"Kristen found you. She got to you before *that* could happen. Still," he grimaces, his eyes studying my face, "you have some cuts and bruises." Brandon's thumb swipes the underside of my wrist. "And your wrist is sprained."

I wince, suddenly feeling the injuries to my face and wrist that he's referencing. The left side of my face is stiff and my wrist throbs.

"It was an attempted rape. When Kristen found you, he was trying to force himself on you, ripping your dress." Brandon averts his gaze, his jaw pulsing with fury, a muscle under his left eye twitching with barely concealed rage.

"But I'm okay?"

"You're okay," he repeats, pulling me close again.

Safe in my brother's embrace, the tears come. An entire tsunami of them that threatens to drown me, that I wish would drown me. At some point, my body grows numb, my mind blank. I cry tears of blackness as icicles form in my veins.

Then, I shut down completely.

───────

DAYS MUST PASS although I don't know if they pass quickly or slowly or at all.

Detachment overwhelms me, numbness consumes me. I attend classes, write an exam, and smile at Sam's jokes. I compliment Kristen as she dresses for a date with Miers. At the appropriate times, I eat lunch, order skinny lattes during breakfast hours, and laugh on cue. I do all of these things and yet, I feel nothing. Only emptiness.

Brandon handles our parents so I don't have to.

Overnight, my internship becomes a safe haven and a living hell. Losing myself in the work is a reprieve and I'm eager to stack files and organize charts, run errands for doctors, volunteer to take coffee orders. But the whispers tucked behind curved hands in the hallways, the averted glances students dart in my direction, the concerned looks nurses bestow on my bent head unnerves me. I feel eyes on me like two pinpricks glued to my back, tracking my every move. Except there are thousands of them and my skin crawls with the unwanted attention.

A week after the "incident" as people are calling it, the news breaks that the person who drugged me, attacked me, sexually assaulted me is none other than Thomas Lawrence, president of the junior class and Astor legacy. His father's recent five-million-dollar endowment to the university has improved his image, spotlighting his family's connections and commitment to the Astor community.

I want to throw up. All the time.

After my last shift of the week, I head to the bus stop when a guy I recognize as one of Cade's teammates approaches me.

"Hey. Lila Avers," he calls out.

Taking a deep breath, I force myself to make eye contact. "Hi."

"Look, I know you don't know me that well but —"

"You play football with Cade."

"Yeah. Listen," he shifts his weight, his eyes narrowing into slits, "whatever went down between you and Tom last weekend is your business. But running around making accusations that could ruin his life is fucked up. You don't have any evidence and you can't deny that you were laughing and flirting and drinking with him." He eyes me, venom in his voice and hate in his gaze. "Fucking Cade Wilkins doesn't make you hot shit. Not every dude on campus wants to bang you. So why don't you do everyone a solid and 'fess up. You drank too much and Tom wouldn't give you what you wanted."

"What?" Is this what people think of me? That I'm lashing out, spreading a vicious rumor because I was rejected? Something in my dead heart shifts, a tiny spark that creates a small crack that I literally feel spreading. Pressing the heel of my hand to my breastbone, I suck in air. "Fuck you."

When the bus pulls up and the doors swish closed, I turn and see Cade's teammate eyeing me. He lifts his left hand slowly and flips me his middle finger.

Slumping down into a seat near the window, I close my eyes, block out the world, and let nothingness wash over me.

33

CADE

Agony.

Lila and I haven't spoken in a week and it's agony.

I'm nearly finished with my chemotherapy and the experience pales in comparison to the hurt I feel for her. I've called, sent countless text messages, even waited outside the hospital a few times, peeping a glimpse of her as she hurries to the bus stop after her shifts. Her eyes are always down, her shoulders hunched, her hair shielding her face from view. She's hurting. She's hurting so badly yet she won't let anyone in. Especially not me.

I miss my bright-eyed Lovely that sparkled with energy, crackled with spirit. In the early morning hours, I smell her coconut scent on my sheets, find a strand or two of her hair stuck to my pillowcase, but when I reach out for her, she's nowhere at all. Completely lost to me. The realization, coming as a throb in my chest, a swift kick to my nuts, an inability to breathe, means I start each morning feeling like complete shit.

It's been a week since Tom sexually assaulted her and the rumors on campus are rampant. Everyone has an opinion on

Glancing past him, I say nothing, searching for my target. Ah, there he is, fourth from the front. Gilly's eyes meet mine, and he takes a step back, preparing to turn away.

"Gilly." My voice is quiet, but even I detect an edge that isn't normally there.

The room falls silent, all banter ending, all movement ceasing. I'm reminded of the night I was injured. The deafening silence of the crowd. Except now it's in my own damn living room.

Gilly steps forward, his eyes darting around to the other guys. No one makes eye contact. "Wilkins."

"We need to talk."

"About what?"

"Privately."

"Whatever you have to say to me, you can say in front of the team." Gilly looks around again, but no one steps in to help him. Instead, the rest of the team keeps their eyes glued to the floor, their bodies shifting restlessly.

"I'd prefer to do this just you and me." My teeth clench until they ache.

"Why don't y'all go out front?" Gogs suggests.

I raise my chin toward the door, and Gilly blows out a loud breath, turning to step outside. Following him, I pull the front door closed behind me.

"What's up?" he faces me, his voice full of bravado he doesn't feel, not with his clenched fists and tapping foot.

"Did you talk to Lila?"

"So what?" he confirms.

"What'd you say?"

"That's none of your business."

"She is my business."

"You guys broke up."

"Answer the damn question."

"Dude, your girl most likely fucked another guy. And then cried assault to deny it. Are you seriously going to step to my face and defend her?"

The muscles in my arm, what's left of them anyway, tingle, tighten, my hand forming a fist. I imagine myself cocking back my arm and knocking his front teeth down his throat. I can see the blood splatter across his chin.

Lila flashes through my mind. Her full lips curving into a smile, the way she tugs on the cuffs of her sweater when she's nervous, her long eyelashes. Her image reminds me of my purpose, ensures I keep my cool. "She was sexually assaulted," I whisper, swallowing the lump in my throat. "I saw her. I was at the hospital." I pound my fist against my chest. "You don't know what happened. You didn't see her. You weren't there. Where do you get off saying anything to her?" I'm inches from his face, staring directly into his eyes.

Gilly shakes his head, taking a step back. "I know Tom. I've known him for three years. He would never do something like that. Lila, you've known her for like a hot minute, man. She was riding a high, dating you, the next big NFL star. Now what? You get sick and the bitch cries assault? Looking for what? Sympathy? Attention? Open your eyes, Wilkins, you're getting played."

My hands are trembling. "Don't ever talk to Lila again. Don't even look at her."

He steps back, raising his hands in a surrender position. "Whatever, man. I don't give a fuck about the bitch."

"Fuck you," I grit out, swinging a fist and hitting him in the jaw. Disappointingly, his teeth stay firmly attached to his mouth. But a sense of satisfaction wells inside as I watch the blood splatter against his chin.

34

LILA

Here I am. A real-life cliché: sexual assault victim crying in the shower like a Lifetime movie.

But I don't want Kristen to hear so the shower is the safest place. No one to see, no one to hear. Of course, the puffiness of my eyelids and the red of my eyes will give me away, but no one will call me out on it.

In fact, I'm sure Kristen and Sam will be relieved that I cried. *She's healing*, they'll think. *She's feeling. Tears are healthy.*

What a crock. I'll never feel whole again.

The entire time Gilly spat accusations at me, all I could think was: Is this what Cade thinks? Does he think I made up a story because I wanted his attention?

The realization that Cade may doubt me cuts the deepest. Because if I need something to believe in, some good to come from this situation, some sign that I may heal and be whole again, then I need Cade.

And I can't have him.

Especially now. How could I ever deserve him?

Turning the water to scalding hot, I scrub my skin. Again

and again and again. Until red marks streak my body, welts forming from the heat.

DANCING THROUGH A MEADOW streaked with wildflowers, I spin in lazy circles. The stars above wink merrily, shooting in delicate designs across the night sky. Exploding like the weeping willow fireworks on the Fourth of July.

A hand touches my arm and slides to the small of my back. A body presses into mine, pushing me down into the grass, hovering over me. Red colors my vision and the peace from earlier is replaced by fear.

The stench of sweat and cigarette smoke fills my nose, a copper taste coats my tongue, and I open my mouth to scream. Except nothing comes out.

Above me, the stars swirl faster, quicker, until nausea rolls through my stomach.

"Shh," a voice whispers right before everything turns black.

Waking with a start, I sit straight up in bed. My sheets are tangled between my legs and my comforter is on the floor. Beads of sweat trail down my neck and chest, and my T-shirt is wet, clinging to my frame.

I suck in air sharply as the nightmare recedes.

I'm fine. I'm okay. I'm safe.

Glancing over at Kristen's bed, I'm relieved that it's empty. Thank God she's been sleeping at Miers's or I would die of embarrassment.

Taking deep, calming breaths, I wait for my breathing to slow. Once I feel steadier, I stand up and remake my bed with fresh linens. Glancing at the clock, it's 2AM which means it's

5AM in Philadelphia. Maura will be waking up for rowing practice. Before I can talk myself out of it, I dial her number.

"Hello?" Her voice is thick with sleep.

"Hi."

"Lila?"

"Yeah. It's me."

"Hey. You okay?"

I sigh. "Not really."

"I know." She pauses. "I'm sorry about everything that happened, Li. I know this is devastating." Her speech becomes more coherent as she wakes up.

I sniffle, no words come out.

"It will take a while for you to feel like yourself again. Don't push yourself. Just focus on one day at a time, okay?"

"Okay."

"Want to just hang out on the phone for a bit? You don't have to say anything. Why don't you try and go back to sleep, and I'll get ready for practice?"

"Can you keep talking?"

"Sure." I hear a rustle of blankets. "As much as I like having a single this semester, I can't wait until you girls are back. Practice has been intense, but the boat is looking really good. I think we'll have a solid season. I met someone. Well, you know him. Do you remember Zack? He was Adrian's best friend. They rowed together. I think I like him because he makes me feel close to my brother. He has a lot of stories about Adrian, and I like hearing them. We went to dinner last weekend," Maura chatters, filling me in on details of her life that I know nothing about.

I want to ask questions, participate in the conversation, but her voice is so familiar and safe, that I'm lulled back to sleep.

AFTER A WEEK OF SLEEPLESS NIGHTS, the dark circles under my eyes are too heavy to ignore. Kristen wears me down and I agree to meet with the therapist that the social worker from the hospital recommended.

"Have a seat wherever you feel most comfortable." Therapist Lisa gestures toward the couch and armchairs in her office.

Taking a seat on the edge of the couch, my eyes dart around the room, snagging on a framed image of colorful butterflies.

"Would you like some coffee, tea, or water?"

"Water would be great." I wipe my palms on my jeans.

Lisa hands me a bottle of cold water from a mini-fridge and takes a seat across from me, crossing her ankles. "What would you like to talk about today?"

Huh? Staring at her in silence, I wait for her to ask a less open-ended question. I'm not prepared to steer this conversation.

"Why don't you tell me more about why you decided to make an appointment?" she suggests.

"My roommate thought it would be a good idea."

"Do you agree with her?"

"I guess so."

"Why do you think your roommate wanted you to book an appointment?"

"I think she's worried about me. I think she and our friend Sam expect me to be a crying, blubbering mess. She's waiting for me to crack and because I'm not, she thinks I'm fragile, weak."

"Do you think you're fragile or weak?"

I shake my head.

"How do you feel?"

"Angry."

"Do you want to tell me about what happened to make you angry?"

I shrug, closing my eyes momentarily, recalling everything I can from that night. "I don't remember much."

"What do you remember?"

Exhaling loudly, I open my eyes and uncap the water bottle.

A raspy voice.

A red flannel shirt.

A tribal tattoo.

And then, it all comes pouring out. Cade's cancer. The harsh, disappointed words from my dad. Cade's rejection. The fight. Crying in the car. Kristen's extra clothes in her trunk. Elm Street. Tequila shots. Dancing. Flirting. Laughing. More drinks. The porch. Smoke. Stars. And a raspy voice in red flannel with a tribal tattoo on his forearm. Tom Lawrence.

A tear trickles down my cheek. I don't brush it away.

Stumbling on the stairs and snagging my bracelet on the carpet. Freezing up. Losing my left shoe. Blackness.

Brandon's face in the hospital. The way his voice spoke to me gently, like I was a child. Cade's wild eyes, briefly meeting mine in the hospital hallway. Sam's anger. Kristen's horror.

Spraining my wrist. The rape kit. Filing the police report at the hospital.

The phone calls and emails and text messages from Mia, Maura, and Emma. Their worry and comfort and tears.

My dad's outrage. My mom's depression.

The ugly rumors and slander circulating around Astor University.

Gilly.

Ugly crying in the shower.

Numbness.

Not wanting to do this anymore.

Exhaustion.

When I finish speaking, my voice is hoarse and I feel so, so tired. Lisa listens patiently, never interrupting, her eyes devoid of judgment or blame.

"Are you sleeping well? Having any nightmares?" she asks.

"Nightmares. Most nights."

"Are you eating?"

"Yes."

"Have you seen Tom at all on campus?"

"No."

"Are you fearful of seeing him?"

Terror seizes my throat at the thought. "Yes. But I haven't thought about it until this moment."

"Would you like to make an appointment to see me weekly from now on? Also, I'm going to recommend that you visit with my colleague, Dr. Abrams. I think he can prescribe something to help you sleep better."

"Okay."

When I leave Lisa's office, I take the bus to the police station. Meeting with a detective, I follow up on the charges I'm pressing against Thomas Reginald Lawrence.

For the first time since the incident, a calmness settles over me, infusing my heart with a degree of acceptance. Suddenly, I'm desperate to go home. I want a break from the nightmare I've been living in. Utilizing my free airline ticket from the start of the semester, I book one return LAX-JFK.

Then, I change into one of Cade's T-shirt's and crawl into bed. His scent soothes me as sleep drags me under.

No black voids. No nightmares.

35

CADE

"How's Lila doing?" I ask Kristen when she and Miers enter the house Wednesday night after dinner.

"Oh, she's in New York," Kristen says, her voice careful, her eyes darting to Miers. "She used her free ticket to head home for Thanksgiving and the long weekend."

"Right." I nod, disappointment flickering in my chest. I imagined us using the tickets together. I thought we'd visit cheesy tourist attractions in the city, barhop around the East Village, and walk the Highline while munching on cupcakes from Crumbs Bakery.

"She needed some time away," Kristen adds, her eyebrows rising, daring me to say something.

"Yeah," I agree, as guilt floods me, washing the disappointment away. Of course she needs an escape from here, a break from the incessant rumors. "How's she doing?"

"Okay." Kristen shrugs, but her tone is wary. Her unwillingness to share information with me stings but I'm also grateful to Kristen. And Sam.

Lila needs real friends right now, especially being so far away from home. As much as I don't want to admit it,

Kristen and Sam are solid and they're looking out for my girl. Even if it means stonewalling me.

Knowing that there's no chance of running into Lila, I attend Saturday's home game. Our team is having a pretty incredible season and we've got a shot at the Rose Bowl. Sitting on the bench during warm-ups, my jersey hanging off my frame, Coach slides into the space next to me.

"Thirty-three."

"Coach."

"A hell of a few months for you," he comments. I can tell by the tone of his voice that he means more than my diagnosis. He means Lila.

"That's one way of looking at it."

"You haven't formally released a statement about your diagnosis yet."

"No, I haven't."

"ESPN and some other news channels have contacted me about an interview."

"Have they?"

Coach grunts.

"What do you think?" I ask him.

"I think you could shed light on a lot of important issues eating at you." He faces the field but his hand curls in the space between us, his fingers clenching.

And suddenly, it's crystal clear. I'm a public figure. At least, I used to be. I'm nearly old news but relevant enough to factor into a news cycle. I'm still a human- interest story that, with the right spin, enough people will tune into.

"Set it up."

"Will do." He stands briskly and claps his hands, yelling out to the team.

Coach doesn't say anything else, but I catch his eye during the third quarter and a look of understanding passes between us. He gives me a curt nod and in it, I read the pride he can't voice.

TWO DAYS LATER, I slide behind the counter next to Joe Simmons and Bobby Palmer on ESPN. Thanks to Coach's connections, the Astor status, and my own story, I'm making news on Thanksgiving weekend.

Clad in one of Miers's suits, which currently fits my shrinking frame better than my own, I remove the baseball cap that hides my baldness. When viewers look at me, I want them to know that I'm not giving up. That I am fighting. For a lot of things.

The makeup girl dusts powder over my face and I grin up at her. "Not much to work with, huh?"

She averts her gaze immediately. *Ah, too soon, Cade.* I'm still adjusting to people not knowing how to act around me.

When the cameras start rolling, Simmons and Palmer introduce me to the show. It's funny really, because for years, I've dreamed of sitting up here, talking football with these men. I figured it could happen as an NFL player or in retirement. And here I am, hopped up on chemo, bald, and about to blow this opportunity to discuss the one thing I care more about than football.

"Today we've got Cade Wilkins joining us. A lot of you may know Cade as Astor University's top running back, and projected NFL draft pick before a recent health diagnosis altered his future plans. Cade," Palmer turns toward me, "I understand there are some things you would like to share with us today?"

This is it. Wiping my palms on Miers's suit pants underneath the counter, I gather all the courage I have and commit to the speech I've been reciting in my mind for the past forty-eight hours.

Stay hungry. Stay focused.

Victory is ours.

Folding my hands on top of the counter, I grin. "Thanks for inviting me to speak on your show, Bobby and Joe. I'm happy to be here and while I love talking about anything football-related, I'd like to discuss a few things outside of the sport.

Lately there has been a lot of speculation about me, the end of my football career, my diagnosis, and a lot of questioning as to why I haven't publicly released a statement. The truth is, I've been trying to wrap my head around it all. Anyone diagnosed with cancer will tell you that the feeling is completely surreal, one of utter disbelief. I didn't believe I was sick, because when I looked in the mirror, I still looked like me." I chuckle, grateful for the grin Palmer throws my way.

"For the most part, I even felt fine. But when I went down in September's game against Stanford, well, that was a blessing in disguise because the stress fracture in my tibia alerted the doctors to my illness. I have Type IIB Osteosarcoma."

"Bone cancer," Simmons clarifies.

"Bone cancer. Man, that was tough to swallow. I was hoping, praying to be a NFL draft pick, and suddenly I was hoping, praying not to die, not to lose my leg, to be able to walk in the future. My focus shifted quickly; my priorities changed overnight. And that's a lot for someone to handle, but also a lot to manage for my team, my friends, and my family." I pause, allowing my words to sink in. "The good news is that my prognosis is pretty favorable. I'm nearly finished with ten weeks of chemotherapy." I point to my bald head. "And I'm scheduled for limb-salvage surgery in mid-December. It looks like I'll live, I won't lose my leg, and I'll walk again. So while losing football has been devastating in many ways, the blow has been cushioned by the alternative. I'm so grateful to be here with you today, to know that the odds are in my favor with my surgery in December, and to have had the chance to play my passion for as long as I have."

"It seems you've learned a lot, grown from this experience, as devastating as it is," Palmer comments.

"Yes sir, I have. But I've also learned some other things."

Simmons waves his hand at me, encouraging me to continue.

"I've learned that there are so many people supporting me. I've experienced an incredible outpouring of love from friends, teammates, acquaintances, fans, and even strangers. It's been amazing to be uplifted by such a community, to feel their love and acceptance, especially during such a hard time. I didn't ask for the support and yet, it was freely given when I needed it the most. But that's not the case for everyone. There are issues occurring every day where people are victims of situations they never asked for, never expected. And yet, they don't receive a tenth of the support, the understanding, the compassion that I have. They don't receive any of the reassurance and acceptance that I have. Maybe they're even doubted, questioned, and blamed."

"What are you getting at, Cade?" Simmons asks, raising his eyebrows at me.

"It's no secret that rape and sexual assault allegations have been increasing on college campuses in recent years."

Palmer lets out a low-whistle, shooting me a look that I don't know how to read. Is he pissed or impressed?

Who cares?

"Victims of sexual assault never expect it to happen to them. And yet, many times, they are shamed, humiliated, made to feel guilty, when they should receive our support, our love, our empathy." I look directly at the camera. "Issues like illness, issues like sexual assault, they are devastating and debilitating, and yet they are handled so differently." Glancing back at Palmer and Simmons, I continue, "I was encouraged to come to your show today, to talk about the loss of my football dream, to discuss my diagnosis, to explain how I've been coping with cancer. Maybe it's because I once was a projected NFL draft pick. Maybe it's because it's a story people can rally behind. Whatever the reason, it's truly an honor." I grin at the guys sitting next to me. "But how many young women or men who are victims of sexual assault at the hands of other students on campuses across America are encouraged to come forward and share their stories, to discuss their feelings, to explain how they're coping with having something stolen away from them? Something much larger than a football dream? And to do so without judgment, blame, and shame? Without universities trying to silence them?" I raise my eyebrows. "I've learned a lot from my cancer diagnosis, but the most important thing I've learned is that I am more than football. And if I can utilize this lesson to help others, then my diagnosis isn't just the end of a dream but the start of a new purpose." I turn back to the camera and wave. "Thanks for having me today."

Simmons comments briefly on my monologue, reiterating the importance of community in sports. Signing off, he waits until the camera stops rolling before reaching over to shake my hand. "Well done, son."

36

LILA

"Oh my God," Maura breathes, kernels of popcorn falling from her mouth. "He loves you."

We're huddled on the living room couch at my mom's house, both in shock, as we watch Cade on ESPN.

Too touched to respond, I stare at Cade, mesmerized by his smile, his stormy gray eyes, the lines of his face. Closing my eyes, I trace his jawline from memory, feel his shoulders bunch under my touch, taste his kiss on my lips.

"That boy is in love with you," Mom agrees.

Maura squeezes my hand. "What are you going to do?"

Opening my eyes, I reach over to swipe Mom's wine glass and take a large gulp.

Does Cade really love me?

After everything that happened?

After everything we've been through?

Watching him on ESPN has left me certain about one thing: he believes me. He doesn't think of me the same way Gilly does. That realization alone calms my heart, makes it easier for me to draw breath.

Cade supports me. But does he still want me?

COMING HOME for Thanksgiving was a good call on my part. The break from campus has offered me the chance to gain some perspective, to stop viewing myself in relation to Cade, his diagnosis, my incident, and start accepting things for what they are: life.

For the first time in years, Mom and I sat down and had an adult conversation, woman to woman. We spent a quiet Thanksgiving dinner together, just the two of us. But it was filled with conversation and laughter and a really good bottle of red wine. We confided in each other and shared stories we've never discussed before. Before bed, Mom made us tea and we ate cookies huddled under a blanket on the couch, watching reruns of *I Love Lucy*. On Friday, Maura surprised me by taking the train up to New York. It's been a perfect homecoming and one I desperately needed.

"Are you sleeping?" Maura whispers, lying next to me in bed, her dark curls piled on top of her head.

"No."

"Are you okay?" Another whisper.

"I'm not sure."

"Do you feel empty? Like a shell of yourself? Or a shadow? Like you can go out and act normal and do everything the way you're supposed to, but not really feel any of it?"

"Yes," I whisper, closing my eyes for a moment. "That's exactly how I feel. It's like I'm going through the motions of my life without any connection to it. I'm numb inside. And yet, everything aches at the same time."

Maura's fingers circle my wrist, and she squeezes. "I know."

"Is that how you felt after Adrian died?"

"It's how I still feel. Although, spending time with Zack is helping." She sobs. "I'm sorry, Lila. I'm sorry this happened to you."

"Me too." I move closer, placing my head next to hers on her pillow. "I'm sorry too. I'm happy you met Zack, that he's helping you heal, to feel again."

She sniffles and I feel a small patch of wetness under my cheek from where her tears disappear into the pillowcase.

"Do you think you'll ever feel whole again? Not so broken?" she asks.

"I hope so."

"Me too."

We're silent for a few moments until Maura's breathing evens out, her slight snore a comfort in the dark. Following her into sleep, I dream about winter and snowflakes falling from a midnight sky.

The cold is a comfort against the heat of my skin. The snow is refreshing, cleansing, washing away the heavy blame and guilt I carry around. Snowflakes settle on my eyelashes and dance through my hair, melting against my cheeks and on the tip of my nose.

Scooping some snow into a plastic cup, I watch in awe as it transforms into cherry ice. Delighted, I giggle, tasting it. Cherry flavor bursts in my mouth, staining my lips red.

"Look!" I yell out to a figure, a hulking shadow some feet away from me. "It's cherry ice!"

The frame of the man turns and a large number, thirty-three, marks his chest.

His jawline is strong.

His eyes swirl like a thunderstorm.

His smile makes my soul sing.

"I'M SO PROUD OF YOU," Mom whispers in my ear at the airport. "So incredibly proud. You do the best you can when you get back to L.A. And then you decide what's best for you for next semester." She pulls back slightly, her eyes meeting mine. "It's your life, Lila. And life is too damn short to be anything but happy."

Leaning into her embrace, I kiss her cheek, breathing her in. Lavender soap. "I love you, Mom."

"Love you too, brave girl. Now go, you'll miss your plane."

Waving to her one last time, I hurry into the security line and make my way to gate A 24. Passing the bar where I met Cade three months ago, I shake my head.

It's crazy how much has happened in three months. I don't recognize the carefree girl with the long blond hair and too much luggage that sat at that bar, ordered a Heineken, and flirted with a hot guy in a gray T-shirt.

But that doesn't mean I don't remember her.

And I want her back.

WHEN MY PLANE lands at LAX, I release a long exhale, feeling determined. I didn't realize how much seeing my mom would settle me, how much Maura's presence would calm me, how much sleeping in my own bed would remind me of me.

The whole version.

Collecting my small suitcase from the baggage carousel, I manage a smirk at the memory of Cade and me here months earlier, him maneuvering my ridiculous amount of luggage with ease, offering to share a taxi.

When I exit the airport, I begin to make my way to the

same taxi line. Looking up, a navy sweater catches my eye, and my breath halts in my throat.

Cade. He's here.

Leaning casually against a pillar just beside the taxi stand.

Dark gray eyes, a thundercloud in each, meet mine with a million unsaid words but shared feelings.

He grins at me and holds up a sprig of mistletoe, shrugging his shoulders.

Before I can overthink, or overanalyze, or question any of it, I release the handle of my suitcase and fling myself into his open arms, snuggling deep into the warmth of his embrace, his sweater pressed against my cheek.

"I missed you, Cade."

He places a small kiss to the side of my neck, inhaling deeply, his fingers catching the ends of my hair. "I missed you more, Lovely."

"I saw you on ESPN."

His body stiffens against mine, his fingers hesitating in my hair before squeezing the nape of my neck.

"Thank you," I breathe out.

"For what?"

"For believing me."

He pulls back, his eyes searching mine. "I never doubted you, baby."

Tears prick the corners of my eyes as I smile, snuggling closer before sliding down his body and resting my ear against his heartbeat.

The whir and buzz of the airport hums around us, but for this moment it's just Cade and me, lost in each other. And it feels reassuringly like home.

When I lean back to catch his eye, he smirks, shaking his sprig of mistletoe. "Happy December, Lovely."

"You remembered."

"I remember everything you've ever told me."

Reaching up on my tippy toes, I press my lips against his. His mouth is warm and tastes like mint. His hands are gentle as they cup my shoulders. I step closer and his grip tightens, his body stiff.

"What's wrong?"

"Lila, I, I'm not trying to assume anything. I–"

"Kiss me, Cade." I arch into his touch and brush my lips against his, begging him to love me back.

His tongue slips inside my mouth and his breath mingles with mine. Cade kisses me with a reverence that strips me bare, a tenderness that cleanses, and a love that makes me whole.

DECEMBER

37

CADE

"I need to tell you what happened. I need to apologize," she whispers in the dark.

While a part of me can't bear to hear the truth, a larger part of me wants to know everything, to absorb all of her pain and anguish, and extinguish it.

There are so many things I wish I could give her. Often, I feel completely helpless. But this, listening when she needs me to, is something I can do. Even if her words tear into me like a chainsaw.

Tugging her closer, I run my fingers up and down the side of her ribcage. "You have nothing to apologize for, baby. And you don't have to tell me anything unless you want to."

"I know. But I, I need to."

I press a kiss to the top of her head. Cars drive down the street, their headlights throwing long shadows across my bedroom wall. Lying in bed, our legs tangled together, the heat of our bodies melding as one, I wait.

"I was angry at you," she starts.

"I know."

"But I was also angry with my dad. Really angry." She

pauses, collecting her thoughts. "I told him I don't want to go to medical school. And he … he was so disappointed. Not angry, yelling, disappointed, but quiet, detached, disbelieving disappointed. I don't know why, but his detachment hurt worse."

I run my lips along her hair in acknowledgement.

"That's why I was so preoccupied. Brandon kept messaging. And my friends. I had emailed Maura, Emma, and Mia after I spoke to my dad and they kept checking in." She sighs heavily. "Anyway, after we fought, I felt desperate. Wild, even. It's like I wasn't good enough for anyone. Not you, not my dad, not my family. And I just wanted to go out and have a good time. Just forget all the crap for one night and drink and dance."

I nod, my cheek rubbing against her forehead.

"I would never betray you like that though." Her voice hardens and she shifts to meet my eyes. "I would never sleep with someone to get back at you. I was hurt and angry and wanted to blow off steam. Not mess around with another guy."

"I barely remember talking to Tom. I was drunk and went to the porch for air. Sure, I was laughing and dancing with guys. I was even flirting. I thought it was all innocent. But I would never act on it." She pauses, squinting one eye like she's trying to recall the hazy details of the night. "I don't remember smoking cigarettes, although someone showed me a photo where I am. I don't really remember much of anything." She raises her wrist. "I remember slipping on a stair and my bracelet catching on the carpet. I remember red flannel. And I remember Tom's tattoo. I remember feeling frozen for a moment. Like I knew something was wrong, but I didn't know how to react to it. I remember feeling the left side of my face burn and sting." She glances up at me again, her eyes shimmering in the moonlight, filled with tears. "I'm sorry, Cade. I'm sorry for hurting you."

"Shh, baby, don't apologize." I pull her flush against my side, needing to feel her warmth, her weight, against me. "I'm so fucking sorry for all of it, Lila. I'm sorry you hurt at all."

"Afterward, when all the rumors and gossip started, when Gilly approached me—"

"He never should have done that. He was one-hundred percent wrong."

"I know. But when he did, I thought … I figured that's how you must feel about me too. That I was just trying to get your attention, to get back at you."

"Not for a second did I believe anything that people were saying. I saw you that night, Lila. I saw you after. And it," I breathe out, my words sticking in my throat like salt water taffy, "it killed me. Your face, I—I hate what he did to you. What he took from you. The self-doubt he created in you. I hate him and I hate myself even more for not being there to stop it. For putting you in a position where you felt like you had to be reckless or blow off steam or whatever. I'm the one who should be apologizing, Lila. Not you. And I am sorry."

"It's not your fault." She places a hand on my cheek, turning my face until my nose brushes against hers. "It's not anyone's fault."

I suck in a ragged breath, anger welling inside of me at the thought of Tom Lawrence putting his hands on Lila, hurting her the way he did. Ice clinks in my chest, expanding until it hurts to breathe.

"I just need you to know that I wasn't trying to hurt you."

"I know that, Lila."

"And I don't know when," her hand flicks between us, "I'll be ready."

The ice clangs loudly in my eardrums.

"There's no rush and no pressure. Ever." Tucking her head under my chin, I hold her close when I tell her, "You and me, we'll figure everything out, how we move forward from here, all of it."

"Okay."

"And you control how things progress with us physically. Whatever you're comfortable with, or uncomfortable with, I just need you to tell me, to be honest. Whatever you're thinking or feeling, say it. Okay?"

"I will."

Quietness settles around us but this time, it's peaceful. The seriousness of our conversation, our doubts and worries now shared, lifts the cloud that has been hanging over our interactions. After several minutes, Lila's light snores punctuate the darkness. Wrapping my arms tighter around her, I hold onto her as I fall asleep.

MY LOVELY IS BACK. It's the biggest relief I've experienced in weeks, which is funny considering my surgery is looming two weeks away. Dr. Somers is satisfied with the outcome of the chemotherapy. Since my tumor shrank, the team of doctors assigned to my case is confident that they will be able to resect the tumor in its entirety.

Too nervous to have any expectations, I focus on the good in my life, my teammates, my family, Lila. With her hair splayed across my pillow each morning, and the spirit of Christmas in the air, it's hard not to feel hopeful for the future.

On Saturday, her brightness bounds through my bedroom door.

"Good morning, sleepyhead."

Reaching out, I pull her flush against my chest, wrapping myself around her.

She twists in my embrace, kissing my forehead, followed by my temple, and then my nose. "I have a surprise for you."

"Really?"

"Yep." She glances at her watch. "But we have to get going. Time is of the essence." She grins, holding out her hand. "And I need your truck keys."

"Hold up. Where are we going?"

"It's a surprise!"

"I'm not really a surprise kind of guy."

"Well, you should be. I'm officially breaking you in. Keys?" Her hand dangles between us, her eyes sparkling, daring me to put up a fight.

Although I don't like surprises, I like everything she likes, so I guess I'll have to adjust. "Keys are on the desk, next to my laptop. I'll be ready in ten. What do I wear to this surprise?"

"Sweats are fine."

"Wow. Giving nothing away."

"You're really bad at this."

I snort.

She reaches forward, her fingertips grazing my cheek. "Eyelash," she explains. Capturing the tiny hair on her pointer finger, she presses it to her thumb. "Finger or thumb?"

I fight the urge to smile. Jared and I used to do this when we were kids. "Thumb."

She opens her fingers and breathes a sigh of relief. "Make a wish."

"I wish—"

"No ..." Her other arm shoots out, her hand clamping

over my mouth. "You can't tell me. Close your eyes and make a wish in your mind."

"Alright."

When I open my eyes, I lean forward and brush my lips against hers. Kissing her slowly, her lips melt into mine, her eyes flutter closed, and a soft sigh escapes her mouth. I catch it, deepening our kiss, my hands pressing into the warmth of her back. She tastes like hope and love and my future all rolled into one.

My wish already came true.

LILA taps the steering wheel as she drives, her large sunglasses hiding her eyes from view. Due to the recent drop in temperature, she's wearing a pair of low-riding jeans, a T-shirt, and a slouchy cardigan that hangs to her knees. I grin at her red Converse sneakers. She is the epitome of a college student mixed with the excitement of a little kid.

"Do we have time to grab coffee?" I ask, pointing to an upcoming Starbucks.

"Sure." She flicks on the blinker and moves into the right lane.

We pull through the drive through and she orders a Grande Vanilla Skinny Latte. I opt for a tall decaf Americano.

She wrinkles her nose. "That's what my dad orders."

"And your opinion of him isn't too great at the moment, huh?"

She shakes her head, pulling her sweater sleeve over her fingers. "Not particularly. Brandon told me that Dad's spending Christmas with Brenda in Aspen. They're going skiing. Brenda is so excited to après," she says the last word in French imitation of her father's girlfriend, who clearly likes to put on airs.

"What do you usually do for Christmas?"

"Brandon wakes me up early, by 6:00 AM. He creeps into my room and then yells and jumps right on my stomach. 'Wake up, Li! Santa came.'" She laughs out loud. "He's such a goofball. We race downstairs, still like little kids. Mom goes all out for Christmas. There's always a massive tree with tiny white lights and lots of gold-accented ornaments. She keeps poinsettias in front of the fireplace, which is already lit, thanks to our housekeeper Lina. Our stockings hang from the mantle. And," she points at me, quirking an eyebrow, "Dad is usually seated in his favorite armchair, a mug of decaf in hand." Clucking her tongue playfully, she leans out the window to receive our drinks from the barista.

"Do you do presents on Christmas Eve or Christmas Day?" I ask, accepting the cups from her.

"One on Christmas Eve, at midnight. The rest on Christmas Day, in the morning. What about you? What are your traditions like?"

Sipping my coffee tentatively, I still manage to burn my tongue. "Careful, it's hot."

"I figured."

"Ha. Christmas at my house was a lot of fun growing up. Jared and I used to decorate the tree with all of our home-made ornaments and strings of popcorn. Mama cooks a massive dinner on Christmas Eve: ham, potatoes, collard greens and cornbread. My dad plays Christmas music for weeks leading up to the big day. And he always makes a toast before we eat dinner that centers on family and tradition. We open most of our presents before we go to bed and save one for Christmas morning, which we open before church. Then, have a huge lunch with my aunts, uncles, and cousins, and just hang out for the day."

"It's like the opposite of mine."

We both laugh as Lila turns back onto the road.

"What are your plans this year?"

"Not sure yet." I shrug, glancing out the window.

I don't want to tell Lila that I'll be alone for the holiday. Mama and Dad are flying out for my surgery, but since it's so close to Christmas they can't take vacation time again two weeks later. I know I won't be cleared to fly so soon after surgery, especially with the risk of infection.

Miers and Hendrix offered to stay on campus, but I refused. They barely get to go home with the football schedule the way it is, and I know how much they enjoy celebrating Christmas with their families. Of course, they both invited me to go with them but I'm not up for attending someone else's Christmas dinner.

Lila reaches over, lacing her fingers with mine. "We could spend Christmas here, together."

"Thank you." I squeeze her hand, turning away from the window. "But you can't do that. You love Christmas and your mom and Brandon need you this year. Besides, what would Mia, Maura, and Emma say? They can't wait to see you."

Her eyes remain focused on the road, her brow furrowing when we pass an exit. "We're almost there," she comments, glancing at me. "Honestly, Christmas isn't going to be the same this year. Dad's in Aspen, Mom wants to visit her sister and my little cousins in Virginia, and Brandon can't take off work. He's spending the holiday with his new girlfriend and her family. I want to stay, Cade. I want to celebrate with you. And trust me, Mia, Maura, and Emma would more than understand. In fact, I think they'd be pretty happy for us."

"You're serious? You really want to stay here?"

"Yes. We can make some new Christmas traditions, you know, mix both of our traditions with some new things thrown in." She glances at me, but I can't read her eyes behind her sunglasses.

"I'd love that. Christmas with you sounds perfect."

"There's just one thing."

"What's that?"

"I need to be out of the dorms before then, so you have to take me in."

Chucking, I lean over and kiss her temple. "You could just tell me you want us to move in together. You don't need to go through this whole Christmas pretense."

"Quit it!"

"Of course you'll stay with me, Lovely."

"Good. This is us." She pulls off the highway and onto a side road that winds for several miles.

"Where are you taking me?"

"To get supplies." She wiggles her eyebrows, hanging a right into a huge lot.

A hand-painted sign welcomes us. Wintergreen Tree Sales.

"We're going to get us a real tree so we can decorate it and start on those traditions," she explains, pulling the truck into a parking spot.

Tossing my head back, I laugh. "You were pretty confident that I wanted to celebrate my favorite holiday with you, huh?"

"Totally."

"This is awesome, Lila. Thank you. I don't deserve you, babe."

"Come on."

Climbing out of the truck, we enter our own type of winter wonderland, eager to choose our first Christmas tree.

38

LILA

"You're spending Christmas with him?" Mia's face fills my screen. "That's amazing!"

"You're not upset, are you? I know you're flying home and—"

"Shut up." She cuts me off. "I'm really happy for you, Li. Plus, he needs you a lot more than the rest of us. We'll just make up for it in January." Her brown eyes crinkle in the corners. "This is awesome news."

"I'm glad you think so."

"We have tons of stuff to catch up on."

"Including the Italiano?"

Mia blushes. "Yes. Especially him. I just wanted to tell you that I'm really happy that things worked out with you and Cade. I have to go now. It's my last final." She rolls her eyes. "But I'll see you in a few weeks, and we will drink all of the wine. I'm bringing home the good stuff and I want to discuss everything in detail."

"That sounds perfect."

"The chat or the wine?"

"Both."

"Agreed. Okay, love you. Talk soon. Give Cade my best and wish him luck on his surgery. Stay strong, sister."

"Thanks, Mia. Good luck on your exam. Talk to you soon."

"Ciao." She hangs up.

With all of my friends and family members on board with my decision to stay, I finally relax. Plans in place, I recline on my bed, scouring Pinterest for Christmas recipes. I've never cooked Christmas dinner before, and I want to make something different so it can be another one of our new traditions. I'm pinning furiously— pumpkin and sage ravioli, linguine and clams, struffoli (Mia sent it), reindeer food, egg nog, etc. —when Kristen and Sam burst through the door.

"Happy End of Semester!" Kristen twirls, her arms raised above her head.

"Today was your last shift?" I ask, closing my laptop.

"Yes! When are you done?"

"Two more days. What about you, Sam?"

"Tomorrow. I'm so over this semester."

I raise my eyebrows. "I thought you were loving the program."

"It's not the program." He sits down on my bed.

"Then what's the deal?"

Sam leans back on his elbow and brushes his glasses up higher on the bridge of his nose. "Chris and I are heading to St Barths for Christmas. I'm ready for some fun and sun and ..." He wiggles his hips suggestively.

"Stop!" I laugh, covering my mouth with my hand. "Good for you."

"It's much needed. What are you doing for the holidays? Kristen told me you're planning to stick around here. Got your own action planned?"

"Something like that. Cade can't fly so soon after his surgery, so we're going to make our own Christmas at the football house."

"I think it will be romantic," Kristen offers, perching on the edge of her bed, her knees bouncing.

"What are you getting Cade for Christmas?" Sam asks.

"I have no idea. I better get on that, huh?"

"Do something thoughtful," Kristen suggests. "Something that shows him how much you care about him."

Sam snorts. "Buy him something baller. He'll appreciate it. He dresses well and has a great ass."

"Thank you, Sam."

He waves his hand dismissively. "You know it's the truth."

"I'll think about it," I tell Kristen.

"I don't know what to get Joe either. Is it too soon?" Kristen wonders.

Sam sits up. "Let's go to the bar. We'll be more creative if drinks are involved."

"Done," I agree, stepping into the closet to find a cardigan. "No, it's not too soon. You met his parents." I respond to Kristen's unanswered question.

I hear her sigh of relief.

"Hurry up," Sam urges, opening the door.

———

THE BAR IS PACKED with end-of-semester revelers. Students huddle outside, smoking cigarettes, and wrapping scarves tighter around their necks.

"It isn't even cold."

"Don't judge," Sam scolds me. "This is the closest we get to winter fashion."

When we enter, we search for an available table. Kristen's eyes widen and she beelines for the bar, managing to snag a corner. Kristen and I occupy the barstools, with Sam standing between us. He rests his elbows on the bar, hunching forward to catch the bartender's attention.

"Okay, I got it. For Chris," Sam begins after we order drinks, "how about I get us a Balinese couple's massage at Eden Rock?"

Kristen snorts, her mojito dribbling out of her nose. The two of us double over in laughter, clutching our sides, and wiping our hands across our mouths to keep our drinks from spraying out. Kristen coughs loudly and the bartender pushes extra napkins in our direction.

"Are you freaking kidding me?" Kristen clears her throat. "Who are you?"

"We're students," I remind him. "We're supposed to eat Raman and furnish our apartments with things we find on the side of the road."

"That is tragic," Sam tells me seriously. "We are adults. We should act like it."

"How can you even afford that?"

"Priorities."

"Well, whatever we suggest now as Christmas gifts for Cade and Joe are going to suck." Kristen elbows Sam.

"Not my fault that you're content living your student life-style," Sam responds, marking air-quotes around the word student.

Kristen rolls her eyes, pushing her shoulder forward to block Sam out of her line of vision. "What are you thinking?" She focuses her attention on me.

"I have no idea. I was so worried about Cade wanting to spend Christmas with me that I didn't even think about presents."

"I'm meeting Joe's extended family."

"What?" Sam interjects, leaning back in. "You're going home with him for Christmas."

"Yeah. And he's coming home with me for New Year's."

"Wow," I whistle.

"I know." She hangs her head. "I have no idea what to get him."

Sam tilts his head to the side, thinking. "Bring two bottles of wine with you in case you visit any family members' houses. Oh and three nicely wrapped boxes of Godiva chocolate." He gives her a pointed look. "You can't go wrong with that and it's a good backup present. For Miers's parents, I suggest a bottle of wine, or scotch. Does his dad drink scotch?"

Kristen shrugs.

"Well, find out. If so, I'll pick one up for you. And then frame a great photo of Miers playing football. Parents eat those things up, and you'll strike a solid balance between sophisticated and sweet."

"Done," Kristen nods. "You're really good at this, Sam."

"I know." He turns to me.

"Am I up?" I ask.

"Kristen was right. For this Christmas, given everything Cade is going through, you better go the thoughtful route."

"Such as …" I prompt.

"I'll have to think about it."

The bartender brings over another round and we celebrate the end of the semester. The conversation shifts to New Year's Eve plans, the first things we're going to do when we get home, and how we're planning to survive next semester without each other.

After an afternoon of day drinking, The Three Amigos retire. We're all exhausted, full, and slightly drunk. I'm settling into bed, Kristen's slight snore puncturing the dark every few seconds, when a thought pops into my mind. I know exactly what to do for Cade's Christmas gift!

Congratulating myself on being brilliant, I drift into a peaceful, dreamless sleep.

39

CADE

"Ready for today?" Nurse Michelle asks around 4AM when she enters my hospital room to check my vitals.

"Morning Michelle. I'm not sure. My girl is meeting my parents for the first time."

She cracks a smile, shaking her head. "Only you would be more concerned about that."

"She's the first girl I'm formally introducing them to. And she's going to have to sit with them for like, eight hours straight during my surgery."

"I see your point. She sounds brave."

"She's fearless."

"Any thoughts on the surgery?" She swaps out an IV bag of fluids.

"Just get through it. Focus on the parts I can control. Get back to the football field."

"Cade." Michelle's voice holds a note of warning and I shake my head.

"Dr. Somers said improbable. Not impossible. Victory is mine, Michelle."

AT 6AM, Mama and Dad arrive, coming to the hospital straight from the airport.

"Oh Cade. I'm so sorry we couldn't be here sooner." Mama scoops me into a tight embrace, running her hand over my head and kissing my forehead. "I miss you, thirty-three."

Clutching at my mama's arms, I hold her tightly, breathing in the floral perfume she's worn every day since I can remember. There's something comforting about the feel of her arms around me, her familiar scent, her voice in my ear. "I'm glad you're here."

"Me too."

When Mama pulls back, Dad hugs me. "You look good, champ." He rolls his forehead to mine, looking straight into my eyes and gripping my shoulders, "You're going to beat this. You hear me?"

"I know."

A timid knock causes all three of us to turn toward the door.

My lovely, my bright spot in a midnight sky, shuffles in the doorway, her eyes dazzling even as she twists her bangle bracelet around her wrist.

"Hey Lovely. Come on in. I'd like you to meet my parents."

She steps forward, "I didn't mean to interrupt, I just —"

Before she can finish her statement, Mama throws her arms around her. "Oh Lila, it's so good to meet you. Thanks for taking such good care of our boy."

"He's the one who's been taking care of me."

Dad steps to Lila and shakes her hand, brushing a kiss across her cheek. "That's how it should be when you find your home team. You look out for each other."

"Good to meet you, Mr. Wilkins."

"Ah, call me Frank."

"Do you mind if I sit with you today?" Lila asks Mama.

"I'd love that. It will give us a chance to get to know each other. Lord knows, we have the time." Mama squeezes Lila's wrist and smiles at me, her eyes flickering with emotion I can't place.

"Mama, Dad, could you give me a minute? Lila, there's something I want to show you." Swinging my legs to the edge of my bed, Mama, Dad, and Lila all rush forward, their arms outstretched, like they're going to catch me before I fall.

"What are you doing?"

"Can you get up?"

"What do you need?"

Chuckling, I shake my head at them. "Good to know you'll all excel at waiting on me, hand and foot. I'm fine, I got cleared by Dr. Somers for this next part." I stand, adjusting the waist band of my sweatpants. "Lovely?" I hold out my hand and tilt my head toward the door. "Take a walk with me?"

Lila's hand fits perfectly in mine, like two puzzle pieces joining together. Leading her down the corridor, we step outside onto a patio, the day waking up around us, the sky still hazy, the wind still cool. Walking to the edge of the patio, I grip the railing.

"Whatever happens today—"

"Cade—"

"No, please, Lila, let me say it."

I look over at her, turning until my back is pressed against the railing, my stance wide. Reaching out, I guide her to stand in between my feet, swiping my thumbs under her eyes as they fill with moisture. "Whatever happens today, whatever the outcome, thank you for getting me through this."

"I didn't. I—"

"You did. You were my rock. You are my rock. Your love and support have kept me going, even on the days I wanted to give up. You've given me a future to hope for and dream about. Maybe it's not the future I thought about before I met you, but now that I have, I want it so badly, Lovely. And that's enough. You're it for me. Bigger than any football dream, greater than any career choice. Regardless of what happens today and tomorrow and next year, I love you, Lila."

"I love you, too."

"This is for you." I hand her a small box, neatly wrapped in gold paper and tied with a purple bow. "It reminded me of you. Elegant and unique."

"Thank you."

"Don't thank me yet. You might hate it."

She snorts, ripping into the package. Lifting the top of the box, her breath catches in her throat. "Cade, this is, it's too much."

"It's not nearly enough."

She holds up the necklace, a thin white gold chain with a diamond snowflake pendant. "I love it. It's beautiful."

"You're beautiful."

"Help me put it on?" She passes the necklace to me, spinning and lifting her hair.

Placing it around her neck, I hook the clasp and press a kiss to her shoulder. "Be my good luck charm today?"

"Always."

She turns back around and steps into my arms. Lifting on her tippy toes, she presses a kiss against my mouth. Palming her cheeks, I kiss her with the sweetness and reverence that she deserves, with the hope I'm too scared to admit aloud.

40

LILA

"I hate hospitals."

"They're the worst," Mr. Wilkins agrees.

"I thought you were in a pre-med program?" Mrs. Wilkins asks.

"That's the irony of it," I admit, passing her a cup of coffee I just purchased in the cafeteria. "Careful, it's hot." Turning, I offer one to Mr. Wilkins.

The Wilkins's and I have only been in the waiting room for two hours, but it seems like eternity. Time in hospitals is strange; it's either too fast to accept or too slow to understand. Either way, sitting in the waiting room is agony.

I'm in agony.

Cade's surgery is estimated to last about four hours. Four long, excruciating hours where a million things could go wrong. The uncertainty eats at my stomach like acid. My hands tremble, my knee bounces up and down. Glancing at Mr. Wilkins, casually thumbing a magazine, his foot crossed against his opposite knee, and Mrs. Wilkins, reading a book, her lips pursed, stresses me further. Why aren't they hysterical? Inside, I'm hysterical.

This room is so similar to the one I waited in the night of Cade's football injury. The same chairs, the same ribbon of blue paint gliding over the white walls. Was that night only three months ago? My entire life has changed in twelve short weeks.

I made a pact to embrace my best life, to have an epic senior year.

And now I'm madly in love with a football player, sitting in a stifling waiting room, wondering what my future even looks like.

"It must be strange being on this side of things," Mrs. Wilkins comments, closing her book, her finger marking the page.

"Sorry?"

"You're studying to a be a doctor, right? I bet it's different on that side of the floor." She eyes the swinging doors to the surgical area. "It must be strange for you to sit here and wait when you're so used to doing."

She's making conversation. She's taking an interest in me and my life. But why did she have to start with medicine? What will she think when she learns I'm not applying to medical school?

"I'm actually thinking of pursuing social work. Maybe with teenagers."

"Oh? Have you always been interested in working with adolescents?" She places her book in her lap, removing her finger as the bookmark.

"No, uh, not really. It was a recent decision." I avert my gaze, watch as my Converse sneaker traces a path in the carpet.

"You've had a tough semester, haven't you?" Her voice is gentle and when I glance up, her eyes flicker with apology.

Heat travels up my neck. "Did Cade tell you?"

"No. He would never share someone else's story like that." She leans forward, placing her book into her bag. "But I know my son. Something must have spurred him to make that speech on ESPN the way he did. When I saw the way he lit up when you walked into his hospital room this morning, well, it wasn't difficult to put two and two together. He's in love with you."

"I love him, too."

"I know you do. And I also know the look you wear when you think no one is watching." Her eyes brim with empathy that causes mine to swell with tears. Placing her hand over mine, she whispers, "I know what having your choices ripped away from you feels like. I'm so sorry that happened to you, sweetheart. I'm sorry for the cruelty you've endured. But I know you alone have been holding Cade together, mending his spirit. Let him be that for you, Lila. Be happy and follow your heart. Choose the path that allows you to heal, be gentle with yourself. Only you know how to make yourself whole again."

Biting the corner of my mouth, I nod, looking down to where her hand rests on my forearm. "Thank you, Mrs. Wilkins."

"No, Lila. Thank you."

"Will you excuse me for a moment?"

"Of course."

Walking out of the waiting room, I hang my head in the corridor. How can Mrs. Wilkins read me so well, understand so much, just by spending a handful of hours in my company? Why can't my own father understand? Support me?

He answers on the first ring. "Lila. I'm so happy you called."

I lean against the blue ribbon on the wall, awkwardly comforted by its presence. "Hi, Dad."

"How are you?" He sounds different, his air of self-assurance deflated.

"I'm doing okay. How are you?"

"Fine. How's Cade?"

"He's in surgery right now. But he's going to be okay."

"Good," Dad grunts.

"I've decided what I want to do after graduation."

He doesn't say anything, so I continue.

"I want to become a therapist. I'm going to apply for a master's program in social work. I want to work primarily with adolescent girls who have experienced sexual assault, abuse, and violence." I swallow, closing my eyes as I rest my head against the wall. "I still want to help people, Dad. I just don't want to do it as a doctor."

A measured pause, followed by, "Oh, well, hmm, good for you, Lila. It's good that you have sorted out your next steps."

Huh? This coming from the man that was adamant about me pursuing a medical degree.

"Are you sure?" I blurt out.

He laughs, but it's strained. "Yes. I'm sure if you are. I didn't realize how much pressure I was putting on you. How much pressure I put on Brandon to be something he's not. After everything that happened to you this semester, after everything that's happened with your mother..." He sighs. "I'm not explaining this well. I guess I'm just realizing I didn't handle a lot of things well, did I?"

Is that a rhetorical question? "Um."

"It's okay." He laughs again. It sounds like wind through a cracked window. "I know I messed up. I don't want to keep pushing you away, Lila. If this is what you've decided to do with your life, well, let me know if I can assist in anyway. I have a lot of contacts in the mental health field."

I snort, rolling my eyes about his "contacts." Instead, I thank him.

"Let me know how Cade pulls through. Brandon says you're spending Christmas in California?"

"Yes, I'll be with Cade."

He clears his throat. "When you're back home, would you like to go to dinner? Just the two of us."

"Yes," I agree. "I'd like that."

"Alright, sweetheart. I'll talk to you soon."

"Bye."

After ending the call, I slide down the wall, along the blue ribbon, until I am sitting cross-legged at the end of the corridor. That was unexpected. I was ready to battle Dad's disappointment, or frustration, or at the very least some condescending remarks. But his support?

What the hell is going on?

Closing my eyes, I think back to the rooftop terrace in New York and recall the faces of my best friends.

It's nearly the end of the semester, I've embraced the College Pact. I've never felt sicker about the future, or more hopeful. Grateful and desperate. Excited and devastated.

The pact was my idea. And I'm proud of myself for embracing its truth.

41

CADE

M y last coherent thought is of Lila. Lila wearing the snowflake necklace, the diamonds throwing the sunlight like a prism.

Lila's golden hair and dazzling eyes.

Lila.

Snowflakes.

Good luck charm.

Victory is mine.

"SURGERY WENT WELL, Cade. We were able to remove the entire tumor. The edges will be tested for remnants of the cancer. Rest now. You can visit with your family in a little while."

Sleep pulls at my subconscious, dragging me into a dream that I desperately want as my reality. Evergreen Christmas trees, snow-covered mountains, cherry ice. And a blond halo hovering over an angel's face. Her smile mesmerizes me, her eyes sparkle, but it's the strength the emanates from her that speaks to me the most.

––––––––––

"Close your eyes and dream of sleep,
    Of clouds and rainbows and ocean deep,
    Of love that shelters and angels that keep
    You safe in dreams of a great big sleep."

Mama's soft voice flows into my consciousness, but my eyelids are too heavy to open. She's singing a song she used to hum when Jared and I were small. Her floral perfume wraps around me like a hug and her presence brings immediate comfort. Breathing out, my throat constricts with soreness and my fingers clench in reflex to the pain.

"Cade?" Mama whispers, her breath cool against my cheek.

My right eye opens slowly, followed by my left.

"Hi, sweet boy," she says, her eyes shimmering with emotion. "You're in the hospital. You did so wonderful, thirty-three. Your surgery was a success. Just rest, don't try to speak."

"Welcome back, Cade." Nurse Michelle hovers over me, pressure squeezes in my right arm. "You did great."

My fingers clasp around Mama's as sleep lulls me under once more.

"See you in the New Year, brother." Miers's hand squeezes my shoulder.

Exhaustion rattles through me. Sleep.

––––––––––

Coconut and summertime wake me up.

"Lovely," I croak the word before I open my eyes.

"Hey there, Cocky." Her fingers brush small circles along my forearm. "You did it."

"You're here."

"Always." Lila holds a straw up to my lips.

I sip the cool water, letting it soothe the burn in my throat.

"How'd it go?" I ask, my eyes drinking in her beauty, memorizing the line of her jaw, the curve of her lips. She's here.

"Very well. They were able to remove the entire tumor. You should be going home in a week or so."

"Home. With you."

She nods, dipping her lips to mine. Whispering across my mouth, she adds, "For Christmas."

She still tastes like cherry ice.

———

Mama and Dad stay as long as they can, but eventually, they have to return to New Jersey. Two days after their departure, I'm discharged from the hospital.

"You're taking these with you." Nurse Michelle reminds me, gesturing to the get-well balloons, floral arrangements, cards, and gifts from friends, family members, teammates, fans, etc. "I didn't realize you were such a big deal."

"You wound me, Michelle," I joke but I'm truly touched by the well wishes and kind thoughts, the overwhelming compassion from so many people.

"Get out of here, Wilkins. And good luck to you."

"Merry Christmas."

Lila arrives an hour later. Wheeling me out of the hospital, we enter the next chapter of our lives together. Even though the embers of our past few months still flicker around us, a reminder of all we've endured, I've never been more hopeful or grateful in my life.

THE FIRST THING I see on Christmas morning is the snowflake pendant shimmering from the soft hollow of Lila's throat.

She's more than my good luck charm. She's my everything.

Stretching, my leg is simultaneously stiff and tender. Ignoring the discomfort, I take a long minute to appreciate the blond waves on my pillow, the rosebud mouth I yearn to kiss, the sweet snore of my lovely.

Not wanting to disturb her, I roll to my side awkwardly, and push myself up into a seated position. Fastening braces to my arms, I hobble to the kitchen and flip on the coffee machine.

While the guys are on winter holiday, Hendrix and Miers moved my bed to the living room so I wouldn't have to brave the stairs each day. It's been four days since I've left the hospital and I'm still adjusting to my new leg, the constant unbalance I feel, the difficulties of performing simple tasks. It's frustrating, but Lila's patience and presence have been positive to my recovery.

Hobbling to the refrigerator, I pull out a carton of eggs and a package of bacon. I'm supposed to be taking it easy but making Lila breakfast on Christmas morning is important to me. It's something Dad always did for Mama. Scrambling half a dozen eggs, I pour the mixture into a pan. Then I fry up some bacon. The aroma is mouthwatering.

When our breakfast is finished, I make two plates and cover them to keep them warm. Opening the cabinet, I chuckle at the snowman and snowwoman mugs. Only Mama would leave personalized "Cade" and "Lila" Christmas mugs.

Setting up our breakfast, I wake up my best Christmas present ever.

42

LILA

"Merry Christmas, Lovely." Cade's gray eyes crinkle, a hat perched on his head.

"Oh! Merry Christmas!" I sit straight up in bed, surrounded by our Christmas creation. Our bed is in the center of the living room to make it easier for Cade to manage without having to take the stairs. Our Christmas tree twinkles next to me, the ornaments colorful and bright. It's the perfect tree, the kind Cade told me that he and Jared had as kids: all mismatched ornaments, vivid colors, strewn tinsel hanging from the branches. Presents are scattered underneath, and two stockings hang on the doorknobs to the kitchen and den, our names written in flourishing script.

"Hungry?" he asks.

"I smell bacon."

"Another new tradition."

"You must really love me."

"More than you know," he agrees, letting me assist him into the kitchen.

Sitting at the table, I grin at my new mug. "Your mom is the sweetest."

Cade nods, lifting his snowman. "To Christmas morning."

"And to the College Pact," I laugh, tapping my mug against his.

"You FIRST." Cade hands me a small envelope with a silver bow attached to the corner. Seated in an armchair, a blanket resting over his knees, his fingers tap out a beat on the armrests.

"Nervous?"

"I hope you like it."

"I'm sure I'll love it." I shake the envelope and Cade grins.

"Open your present, babe."

Sliding my finger under the envelope flap, I pull out the folded paper inside and glance at Cade.

"Read it." He tosses a throw pillow at me.

Unfolding the paper, my heart melts. Cade wrote me a letter.

Dear Lila,

Merry Christmas! I'm so grateful to celebrate today with you. After everything we experienced and endured this semester, sharing today with you makes it all worthwhile.

When we met four months ago, I never thought we would be here today, lost in our own winter wonderland. I'll never walk into another airport without remembering the first time I saw you. I'll also never drink another Heineken without remembering how your face lit up when you talked about "smiling e's." You've given me every single reason to smile.

You've also made many sacrifices to give me a beautiful Christmas, a whole heart, and an optimistic outlook despite my long recovery ahead. People always say long-distance relationships don't work, but most people don't experience what we have and come out of it stronger.

I want to know your life, Lila, the same way you've embraced mine. I want to meet your friends and family and share the future with you by my side.

As a first step, let's go home, Lovely.

Mia, Maura, and Emma will be waiting for us at Marco's Ristorante at 7:00 PM on January 7 in New York City. I can't wait to meet them and take you back to where we first met – New York.

I love you.

Cade

"Are you serious?"

"We fly out on January 6. Dr. Somers already cleared me."

"I can't wait to introduce you to my friends!"

"I can't wait to meet them. And be back on the East Coast with you."

"Thank you." Pure love for this man warms my chest as I lean forward and kiss him. I could kiss him for days and it will never be enough. Treading the line of no return that we're not allowed to cross until Cade is cleared for sex by Dr. Somers, I rip my mouth from his. Grinning, I hand him his gift. "I hope you like it."

Cade tears into the paper like a proper kid on Christmas morning.

When he sees the book, his hands freeze, his eyes dart to mine.

"Lila." It's a breath of air, of awe.

Opening the scrapbook, he turns the pages slowly, his eyes drinking in the highlights of his entire football career, from tossing a ball in the yard with Jared to the game against Stanford. Pages of photos, newspaper clippings, and stats are interspersed with quotes from the coaches who trained him over the years, teammates he played with, and even opponents.

"Wow." Tears swell in his eyes as his fingers brush over a blown-up photo of him and Jared, each of them holding up one side of a Mustang jersey that reads: Wilkins, 33. It was taken the day he accepted to play at Astor.

"Do you like it?"

"This is the best gift I've ever received. Thank you. It's priceless. Like you." He gestures for me to move closer and brushes a sweet kiss across my mouth. "Now back away because I want nothing more than to kiss you senseless, slide into you, and work you over until tomorrow and we both know that can't happen."

Snorting, I pull away, balling up the discarded wrapping paper and adding some space between us. "I guess our first Christmas was a success?"

"I'll let you know after dinner. What are you cooking again?"

"Cade!"

"Lila."

"Don't get cocky."

"Stay lovely."

"He loved it, right?" Emma asks, chewing in my ear.

"What are you eating?"

"Pretzels. Don't get sidetracked. Tell me about his reaction."

"He loved it."

"Yay! I knew it! I can't wait to see you in a few weeks."

"I know. I can't believe you guys planned this."

"Hold on. I'm drinking." Emma pauses. "Okay. Yeah, well when Cade Facebook messaged us, we knew for sure he's the real deal. Plus, we need to meet him. I hardly know any hot athletes, so this is a big deal for me."

"Clearly, the main purpose," I joke. "It will be a good night."

"The best. Okay, I got to go. I'm still at my Aunt Sophie's and her little munchkins are waiting not-so-patiently to play Clue." I hear the squeal of little kids laughing.

"See you on January 7. Send me pics of your outfit options."

"Done. Bye, Li."

"See you."

I hang up with Emma and squeal myself. I'm going home in a few weeks. With Cade!

JANUARY

43

CADE

The bitter cold of New York in January bites my skin the moment Lila and I exit the airport. The ground is wet with melted snow and brown slush. Keeping my eyes trained on the pavement, I maneuver carefully to the taxi line. Lila shivers in her cardigan and wraps her scarf tighter around her neck. I wish I could pull her into my chest and warm her up.

We both lack appropriate winter clothing and are bundled in multiple layers until we make it to her mom's house where real winter gear awaits.

Stowing our luggage and my braces in the trunk of a waiting cab, Lila and I slide inside. She gazes out the window, her soft blond waves falling over her shoulders. Watching her twist the sleeve of her cardigan around her wrist, I grin, knowing she's lost in thought.

In four short months, my life has drastically changed. Taking the field for my last first game at Astor, I remember the weight that settled around me knowing it was the last time I would open a season as an Astor player. That feeling, that bittersweet certainty, is etched into my memory.

But it's nothing compared to the permanent certainty I have now. Because my lovely is my real last first. She's the only last first that counts. The last first girl I ran game on. The last first girl I asked out on a date. The last first girl I kissed until she consumed me. The last first time I willingly entrusted my heart into the safekeeping of another person.

And now, I just want her to be my always.

EPILOGUE

CADE

Two Years Later

"Congratulations to the graduating class!" The speaker announces as wild applause breaks out.

Standing, I whistle, cheering for my lovely.

"I'm so damn proud of her," Lila's dad says, standing next to me.

"Yeah. Completing a master's in social work is no joke."

"And from NYU. You know, the Silver School for Social Work is very competitive."

I nod, catching Brandon's eye on the other side of his dad. We both cough our laughter into our fists. Turning back toward the graduating class, I clap harder when Lila's name is announced.

The past two years haven't been easy as Lila and I both struggled to reframe our futures. It took just over a year from my surgery for me to walk into a gym for the first time. Miers and Hendrix accompanied me and under their encouragement and tough love, I rehabbed my leg.

Shortly thereafter, I accepted two jobs that keep me as

close to the football field as possible while also filling me up with a sense of purpose I never anticipated experiencing again.

As the head coach of my high school's football team, I spend my afternoons with a bunch of hungry teenagers, breathing in freshly-cut grass, the feel of a pigskin in my hand, sharing my love for the game of football.

When I'm not actively coaching, I'm talking. Hosting my own sports show, *Real Talk*, on ESPN has been the chance of a lifetime. Discussing sports, especially football, has always been a passion of mine. But adding in the controversial and important topics in the sports realm that are often overlooked at the collegiate and professional levels has fueled me with purpose. My show covers real issues that affect real athletes, such as eating disorders among athletes trying to cut weight in sports like rowing, wrestling, and dance, the wage disparity between male and female athletes, particularly in the NBA, and the use of performance-enhancing drugs.

On *Real Talk*, we discuss a lot of issues that are important to athletes, viewers, and fans, but also to me. I love shedding light on controversial topics that most universities and professional sporting associations don't want to delve into. Sure, it means a lot of people don't like me.

But I don't care about being liked as much as I care about doing something that makes me feel whole. Who knew that would be giving back to a community I love?

Well, I guess Lila knew. Because she's embraced her calling in social work with both hands, dedicating her time and energy to assisting adolescent girls, mostly victims of sexual assault and abuse.

Every morning, her kiss fills me with optimism and each night, her hand in mine showers me with gratitude.

I am a lucky man; I know it.

Clearing my throat, I glance at Lila's dad, Brandon, and Lila's mom, now happily remarried as Mrs. Lee.

"What's up Cade?" Brandon asks, a smirk glancing off his mouth.

Pulling the small black box from my pocket, I open it and flash Lila's family the one point five carat, flawless, princess cut diamond engagement ring inside.

"Oh, that's beautiful," Lila's mom gasps.

"I'm going to propose to Lila."

Lila's dad quirks a brow. "You're not asking my permission, are you?"

"I'm not for asking anyone's permission, sir. But I'd like your blessing."

"You're still a cocky son-of-a-bitch." Brandon laughs, flashing me the thumbs up. "Make my sister happy, man."

"Always." I glance at Lila's parents, noting the tears shimmering in Lila's mom's eyes as she nods at me. Turning toward Mr. Avers, he clasps me on the shoulder and shakes my hand.

"Welcome to the family, Cade."

"She hasn't said yes, yet," I remind them.

The three of them look at each other and burst out laughing, turning their attention back toward the field.

Grinning, I look for my lovely, desperate to make her my wife.

Epilogue - Lila

"You're serious?" I gasp, my eyes swinging from the blinding engagement ring to Cade's gaze. His eyes, a shade lighter than a rainstorm, shine with so much love for me, I stagger back a step.

He frowns. "Did I misread —"

"Yes!" I shriek, rushing him. Throwing my arms around his neck, I pull his mouth to mine and kiss him. "Yes, yes, a million times yes."

His mouth splits into the biggest smile I've ever witnessed as he teeters on his knee. "You scared me. I thought, well, it doesn't matter. I can't wait to make you Mrs. Wilkins." His hands grip my waist, pulling me flush against him, as we fall to the ground.

"Good, because I've been waiting for you to be my husband for a long time." I straddle him, relieved it's just the two of us in this patch of green in Central Park.

"Clearly."

"Still Cocky as ever."

"Always so damn Lovely. Say you'll be mine." He kisses my nose, his eyes darkening with desire.

"Always."

THANK you so much for reading *The Last First Game*! I hope you loved Lila and Cade's story.

Do you adore brother's best friend romances? Do you live for emotional and angsty reads? If yes, don't miss Maura and Zack's romance in *All the While*.

AN EXCERPT FROM ALL THE WHILE

Maura

I wasn't always promiscuous.

In fact, I never slept around until my twin, Adrian, disappeared from my life.

Before that, I cared too much about upholding the values our parents raised us with to ever have a slew of one-night stands. But when he stopped playing by the rules, I figured why shouldn't I?

And that's how it started.

The drinking, the sex, the painful loneliness that eats pieces of my heart and gnaws at my soul. Even when I'm surrounded by my rowing team or hanging with my best friends, Emma, Lila, and Mia, I'm so alone it hurts to breathe in too deep.

Like if I do, I'll shatter the façade I'm trying so hard to keep up.

So, I drink.

Wine. Vodka. Tequila.

Anything to numb my body from absorbing the shock of Adrian's loss.

Anything to numb my mind from processing that he's gone, from addressing the anger I'm harboring over his death.

Because the truth is, I'm furious at my twin for leaving me behind.

But how can you stay angry at a dead person when the rest of his world placed him on a pedestal?

My mom can't mention his name without tears welling in the corners of her eyes. My dad prefers to pretend that everything is fine.

And so I'm utterly alone.

Alone in my thoughts, alone in my grief, and definitely alone in my anger which, some days, threatens to consume me.

To embrace the numbing detachment I've come to rely on, I need to drink.

I need to inhale the calming sweetness of Marlboro Menthol Golds like no athlete before me ever has.

I need to have lots of deliciously mind-numbing sex with random men.

In the mornings that follow, I wash their scent off of my skin and pretend the night before never happened. And if I'm really lucky, I can hardly remember the night at all.

The only thing I don't touch, never have, never will, is drugs.

Because as much as I miss my brother, I'm furious with him for taking his own life. Sure, he didn't intend to at the time. But isn't an overdose just as selfish as suicide?

I keep my head down and my grades up. I attend rowing practices on time, dig into each and every catch, my hair tucked into one of Adrian's old baseball caps, my sunglasses hiding the void in my eyes. And even though everyone knows something is wrong, something is off, no one can figure out what it is.

Until Zack, Adrian's best friend, intervenes.

I just don't know it yet.

"Are you awake?" Mia's whisper cuts through the silence of her childhood bedroom. She's sitting up, her elbow propped against the pillows resting in front of her headboard.

"Who?" Lila asks sleepily.

"Any of you?" Mia whispers.

"Why are you whispering? We're all obviously awake." Emma's voice booms. She sits up in bed next to Mia. I can just make out her shadowy silhouette from my spot on the air mattress at the foot of the bed. "Right, Maura?"

"I am now," I answer.

"Do you think it's a good idea?" Mia asks.

"What?" Lila sits up next to me. The mattress dips dangerously low on my side as she shifts her weight. She runs her fingers through her golden waves lazily. "Is what a good idea?"

"Going to Rome?" Mia's voice is still a whisper.

"Yes!" We all exclaim in unison. Lila flops back down next to me and the air mattress lurches under my shoulder blades.

"It's going to be great, Mia, you'll see," Emma says reassuringly. "This semester, it's going to be epic. We're all going on such exciting adventures!" Her voice is alive with the anticipation of the future, of the unknown. An awkward silence settles as my best friends acknowledge that I'm not going on an adventure.

I'm not going anywhere.

"And you're going to win Dad Vail this year!" Emma tries, overcompensating with her enthusiasm.

"Yeah, it will be great."

"Seriously, Maura," Lila picks up where Emma leaves off, "the pact ... it's about pushing past our comfort zones, erasing some of those boundaries that have been restricting us. It's about having fun and letting go, for one semester. You can do that from anywhere." Her voice holds a note of a challenge that irritates me.

Stupid college pact. We all agreed earlier today, while eating pizza and drinking sangria at one of Mia's favorite New York restaurants, that we would live it up this semester. Be wild, be courageous, be brave, try new things, blah, blah, blah. And it makes sense. It really does ... if you're Mia, Emma, or Lila.

They're going on real adventures, leaving McShain University behind. They're starting new chapters with new people in new places. Tomorrow morning Mia flies to Rome, Italy to study abroad. Emma is heading to Washington, D.C. for an internship on Capitol Hill. And Lila, who keeps joking about the killer tan she's going to sport and the hot guys she's going to meet, is participating in a medical internship through Astor University in California. They're all going on adventures, already pushing past their comfort zones, moving the invisible lines that demarcate their self-imposed boundaries.

But I'm not.

Nope. Not me.

I'm heading back to our campus at McShain University, still in Philadelphia, back to rowing. I'm not being wild, or courageous, or brave. Unless you count hitting up my old neighborhood to slum it with some of the guys, like Hector, who I know still kick it there.

Sighing heavily, I turn so Lila won't detect the tears brimming in my eyes. I'm going to be lost without these girls. Even at my worst, things seem manageable when they're around to keep me in check. But now, with all of them gone and wrapped up in the excitement of their new lives, I really will be on my own. Completely alone.

"Sure," I say into the silence, trying to sound confident.

No one buys it.

Mia turns on her reading lamp and the light bathes half her face in a warm glow. "Trust me, Maura, if I can get on a plane to Rome tomorrow morning, you can have an incredible semester and an even better start to the season."

"I know."

Because this is what I always wanted, isn't it?

This year, this season, is the culmination of everything I've worked for: endless hours of practice in the freezing rain, summer camps, two-a-days, torn hands coated with blisters the size of grapes, stress fractures layering my ribs. All of it was for this season so McShain University's women's rowing would be the best, number one, team in the United States.

It's what we always dreamed about. Adrian and me. He rowed for LaFarge University, also in Philadelphia. Being near him is one of the reasons I chose to attend McShain. That, and the full-ride scholarship. Still, being close to Adrian was an important determining factor. I mean, we're twins; we've practically been joined at the hip since before we were born. It's funny, really, people always think twins have some sort of special connection or bond. I never thought about it before or gave the idea much merit. Except now that he's gone, it's as if half of me is missing. We spent our whole lives growing together, and I don't want to move forward on my own. Alone.

Now that he's gone, I don't know how to keep holding on to half a dream.

Moments of silence tick by, and I hear Emma's soft snore. Lila snorts next to me, and Mia chuckles. Keeping my eyes closed, I feign sleep as they continue to talk about their semesters in new places.

Listening to their chatter, nerves spike in my bloodstream.

When did we grow into adults?

When did everything change?

Any why am I always being left behind?

Read *All the While* **now!**

ACKNOWLEDGMENTS

Hey there!

Re-writes and re-launches are wild! The College Pact Series has such a special place in my heart because it draws heavily from my own college experiences – I studied abroad in Rome, rowed my freshman year, and interned in Washington DC. Clearly, California was more of a bucket-list item – and it still is! I fell in love with Lila and Cade when I first wrote them and all over again when I revamped *The Last First Game*.

So many thanks and appreciation –

Kate Farlow at Y'all That Graphic - I am in love with these new covers! Thank you for making them pop!

Melissa Panio-Peterson – A million thank yous for your time, support, and beautiful graphics! I love working with you.

Patrick Hodges - thank you so much for proofing this book at the last minute and turning it around in record time! You're the best!

All the wonderful writers at Romance Author Mastermind 2018 – If it wasn't for all I learned from you awesome ladies, I wouldn't have revamped this series and I am so, so glad I did. Thank you for the insight, encouragement, and invaluable advice. You all are rockstars!

Give Me Books Promotions – it is always such a pleasure working with you all! Thank you for the support!!

Of course, all of the incredible bloggers and bookstagrammers – THANK YOU! Thank you for sharing books that you love and thank you for falling in love with characters as much as the authors do! A special thanks to Ola, Chloe (bibliophilechloe), Sandra (cofffeeandbooks), Dana, Melanie, and Heather - and Alexis! - (a book nerd, a bookseller and a bibliophile), Margaux (bookaholicmargaux), and Robin and her fabulous group (Books, Boys, & Booze) – your support has meant so much to me.

To all the readers – I hope this book encouraged you to reminisce about your college adventures – and loves! I am so grateful to you.

To all of the wonderful friends, classmates, professors, and strangers I met through my own college experience – thank you for contributing to my journey.

To my family and friends, near and far – thank you for believing in me.

To my home team – Tony, Aiva, Rome, and Luna – love you all the world and then some.

Happy Reading!

Xo,

Gina

ALSO BY GINA AZZI

The College Pact Series:

The Last First Game (Lila's Story)

All the While (Maura's Story)

Me + You (Emma's Story)

Kiss Me Goodnight in Rome (Mia's Story)

The Kane Brothers Series:

Rescuing Broken (Jax's Story)

Recovering Beauty (Carter's Story)

Reclaiming Brave (Denver's Story)

My Christmas Wish

(A Kane Family Christmas

+ *One Last Chance* FREE prequel)

Finding Love in Scotland Series:

My Christmas Wish

(A Kane Family Christmas

+ *One Last Chance* FREE prequel)

One Last Chance (Daisy and Finn)

This Time Around (Aaron and Everly)

Second Chance Chicago Series:

Broken Lies

Twisted Truths

Saving My Soul

Healing My Heart

Standalone

Corner of Ocean and Bay

ABOUT THE AUTHOR

Gina Azzi writes Contemporary Romance with relatable, genuine characters experiencing real life love, friendships, and challenges. She is the author of The Kane Brothers Series, The College Pact Series (re-launching summer 2019), and Corner of Ocean and Bay. All of her books can be read as stand-alones.

A Jersey girl at heart, Gina has spent her twenties traveling the world, living and working abroad, before settling down in Ontario, Canada with her husband and three children. She's a voracious reader, daydreamer, and coffee enthusiast who loves meeting new people. Say hey to her on social media or through www.ginaazzi.com.

For more information, connect with Gina at:

Email: ginaazziauthor@gmail.com
Twitter: @gina_azzi
Instagram: @gina_azzi
Facebook: https://www.facebook.com/ginaazziauthor
Website: www.ginaazzi.com

Or subscribe to her newsletter to receive book updates, bonus content, and more!